M000197207

SVEND ÅGE MADSEN

DAYS WITH DIAM: or LIFE AT NIGHT

Some other books from Norvik Press

Sigbjørn Obstfelder: *A Priest's Diary* (translated by James McFarlane)
Annegret Heitmann (ed.): *No Man's Land. An Anthology of Modern Danish Women's Literature*
P C Jersild: *A Living Soul* (translated by Rika Lesser)
Sara Lidman: *Naboth's Stone* (translated by Joan Tate)
Selma Lagerlöf: *The Löwensköld Ring* (translated by Linda Schenck)
Villy Sørensen: *Harmless Tales* (translated by Paula Hostrup-Jessen)
Camilla Collett: *The District Governor's Daughters* (translated by Kirsten Seaver)
Jens Bjørneboe: *The Sharks* (translated by Esther Greenleaf Mürer)
Jørgen-Frantz Jacobsen: *Barbara* (translated by George Johnson)
Janet Garton & Henning Sehmsdorf (eds. and trans.): *New Norwegian Plays* (by Peder W.Cappelen, Edvard Hoem, Cecilie Løveid and Bjørg Vik)
Gunilla Anderman (ed.): *New Swedish Plays* (by Ingmar Bergman, Stig Larsson, Lars Norén and Agneta Pleijel)
Michael Robinson (ed.): *Strindberg and Genre*
Michael Robinson : *Strindberg and Autobiography*
Irene Scobbie (ed.): *Aspects of Modern Swedish Literature*
James McFarlane: *Ibsen and Meaning*
Robin Young: *Time's Disinherited Children* (on Ibsen)
Egil Törnqvist and Barry Jacobs: *Strindberg's Miss Julie*
George Brandes: *Selected Letters* (selected and edited by W.Glyn Jones)
Jacob Wallenberg: *My Son on the Galley* (edited and translated by Peter Graves)
Kjell Askildsen: *A Sudden Liberating Thought* (translated by Sverre Lyngstad)
Johan Borgen: *The Scapegoat* (translated by Elizabeth Rokkan)

The logo of Norvik Press is based on a drawing by Egil Bakka (University of Bergen) of a Viking ornament in gold, paper thin, with impressed figures (size 16x21mm). It was found in 1897 at Hauge, Klepp, Rogaland, and is now in the collection of the Historisk museum, University of Bergen (inv.no. 5392). It depicts a love scene, possibly (according to Magnus Olsen) between the fertility god Freyr and the maiden Gerðr; the large penannular brooch of the man's cloak dates the work as being most likely 10th century.

Days with Diam
or: Life at Night

By Svend Åge Madsen

Translated by W. Glyn Jones

Norvik Press
1994

About the author:
Svend Åge Madsen, born 1939, stands today as one of Denmark's most important experimental novelists. Concerned with the unstable or illusory nature of reality, he is a master of the fantastic, skirting round realism, but never entirely realistic. For him, time, place, human nature are all indeterminate concepts, all tending to dissolve and re-emerge elsewhere in a different form.

About the translator:
W. Glyn Jones is Professor of European Literature at the University of East Anglia, Norwich. Among his publications are two books on the Danish writer Johannes Jørgensen as well as monographs on the Faroese novelist Willian Heinesen and the Finland-Swedish Tove Jansson. His translations include Georg Brandes' letters, Villy Sørensen's *Seneca* and William Heinesen's *The Black Cauldron*.

British Library Cataloguing in Publication Data
Madsen, Svend Åge
Days with Diam: or Life at Night
I. Title II. Jones, W. Glyn
839.81374 [F]
ISBN 1-870041-26-7

Set in 11 pt Garamond antiqua.
First published in 1994 by Norvik Press, University of East Anglia, Norwich, NR4 7TJ, England
Managing Editors: James McFarlane and Janet Garton

Norvik Press has been established with financial support from the University of East Anglia, the Danish Ministry for Cultural Affairs, The Norwegian Cultural Department, and the Swedish Institute.

Printed in Great Britain by Biddles Ltd, Guildford, Surrey.

Contents

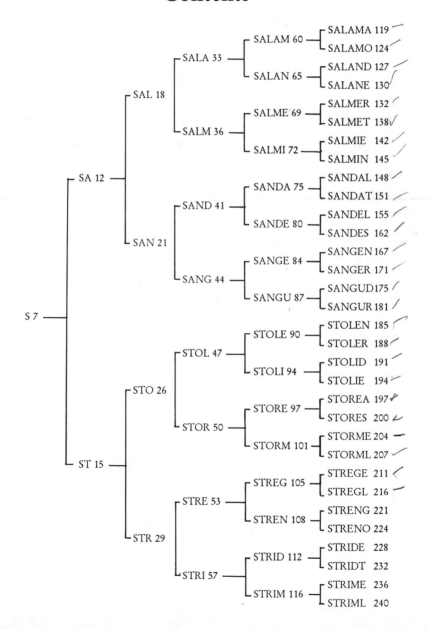

S

The world and the contents of my mind cannot be torn apart. No power, no event can do that.

Thus I write on the paper before me. What feeling does it awaken in me?

Nevertheless, I cannot keep the two phenomena united, there seems all the time to be some discrepancy between them, all the time there is something I'll call the world, all the time there is something I'll call my fancies.

I cannot go on, cannot believe in it any longer.

She is never completely absent. Even when I think I am most engrossed in my writing she is here somewhere, somewhere behind my thoughts.

When I have read through these last words of mine, I add in the margin: Too pompous, needs to be reformulated and given a comic or elegant touch. At the same time I know that I shall never manage to carry out this suggestion.

I take the two quite disparate books from the writing desk, fling Lanson's *What the World Showed* into a corner, and put *The Man on the Road* by Cloy Marel up on the bookshelf.

At the top of the sheet I write in my most contemptuous handwriting: The Twisted Paths of the World. Then cross out World and replace it with Mind.

'I'll probably not come,' I said to her.

'No, that's obvious,' she replied.

I can intonate her words in seven different ways. I try them all out to keep myself in training. The whole gamut, from the one suggesting: 'I didn't expect it of you in any case, lazy as you are', through: 'I'm sorry about that', to: 'Oh, thank goodness'.

Silence seems to be prowling all around me. Even the sea is silent tonight. There is nothing but a few embers left in the fireplace. If I put on a little more wood it might mean that after all I had plans for going across to her place and wanted to be sure of finding a warm room on my return.

When I brush aside all thought of her it is the happening that imposes itself on me. Have I any sense of guilt? Or do I think it would be interesting if I had a sense of guilt?

If not, why am I starting to give an account of it?

From here it is a good half hour's walk to Dahle. As a rule when I come here I bring with me what I need in the way of food and so on, but I like to walk up to the little town to see people, have a brief talk to them. They smile and nod, I make the amiable comment I have prepared in advance.

I like the dialect here, listen to people as they talk to each other. On a few occasions I have overheard a peculiar turn of phrase: 'We haven't done anything at all for the past week, it's been as monotonous as Toran Lynde's life.'

I was curious and tried to discover the background to the expression. Finally got at it, although people don't say more than they want to.

The man referred to in the expression is still alive, a middle-aged man with a little farm on the outskirts of the village. He also works as a carrier occasionally to supplement his living. He is said always to have been very ordinary and never to have undertaken anything of note.

But a few years ago he must have come across the well-known person retailing the trivial assertion that there is at least one story to be told about everyone: their own.

'No,' Toran is supposed to have replied here.

At any gathering of people after that day he discovered that an account of his story-less life made him of immediate interest.

Before long it was expected of him that he should explain how insignificant he was, just as another person had to tell of his last visit to the tax office, and a third to mimic various well-known personalities.

Lynde managed to establish his view of himself in his circle of acquaintances, hence the currency of the phrase in that district. For instance, the most damning comment to be made on a film is something like: 'Don't bother to go and see it, it is as dull as Toran Lynde's daily life.'

When I first met him he had just been discharged from hospital. One fine day, of course, he had been run into by a car and broken his leg. He took this event in good part: who doesn't have a road accident nowadays; it would almost have been noteworthy if he hadn't.

To me he happily made his assertion that there was no story to be told about his life, but otherwise he had little to say.

One Saturday evening, at his weekly game of cards, he is said to have had twelve spades (the thirteenth was a diamond) in one hand. He found this amusing. A hand like this is admittedly unlikely, but wouldn't it be unlikely for nothing unusual ever to happen just to him? One person has three children all born in turn on the very same day of the year; another meets someone else called exactly the same as he and looking like him into the bargain, a third, as a child, pulls out a stone from the soil and throws it up on the air, and when it falls down it lands in the very the hole from which it was taken.

This is how Toran Lynde defended his life, about which no story could be told.

On a certain occasion I happened to mention the man and the curious turn of phrase to one of my colleagues, who unfortunately is something of a scatterbrain.

It does you good to tell a story. The words slip out almost of their own accord, and your thoughts no longer force themselves on you.

My meddlesome colleague turned up one day at Toran Lynde's home. He had an absolutely marvellous idea: he would write a documentary novel based on his life. Or perhaps even better: a film critical of social conditions.

Lynde is said to have been more upset than ever before in his story-less life. He alternately remonstrated and pleaded to be spared. How on earth was he to keep his end up now if he had the unusual experience of becoming a famous character in a novel? Everyone was going to maintain he'd been lying if his life was really so interesting as to be worth filming.

My colleague immediately abandoned his scheme, but that didn't mean the end of the story. Today I met an extremely harrowed Toran Lynde, who was unusually communicative. We sat down together by the wayside. After directing a violent attack on authors in general, he told the following story.

After the offer, he had felt so terribly upset, bereft of all his past life, that he decided to commit suicide. He had already planned this to take place under dramatic circumstances, when he suddenly envisioned the headlines this would produce in the press: Monotonous Life Ends In Magnificent Death, or Melancholy Life Worthy Of Tragedian.

He decided not to die in this way and looked for another. He could make his suicide look like murder: He was an insignificant person, with no enemies and no friends – and yet he was murdered – why?

I hadn't the heart to tell him that it sounded like the back cover of a detective novel rather than a newspaper headline.

He had tried to waste away, to die a trivial death. He had tried holding his breath, but he drew it with a gasp when he had realized that this, too, would make him noteworthy.

'I shall have to go on living with my fate,' he said heavily. 'But what can I do? Can I change myself, kick over the traces, drink, women, affairs? The man who fundamentally changed his life.'

'Or shall I go on with my monotonous, obscure life in which my great delight, my task among my friends, was to tell them about my lack of a story. But I can't, I can't escape the ridiculous proposition: The man who rejected fame and perpetual limelight in favour of obscurity and insignificance.'

I had the greatest difficulty in calming down this depressed man who was convinced the fault was mine.

'I won't stand for it. I won't be forced to live as a story. I want my own life, that's all, just my own life. And it shall not be as you lot want it. I want it back. You told him about me, you had no right to do that. You must do something about it. You must do something straight away. People have already begun to talk about me, they're telling long stories about me. Get it stopped, you must do something.'

Of course, there is nothing I can do for him. The trouble is of course that he has been living for too long on a wrong premise. One would have to reach far back into his life in order to do anything for him.

There is still enough time left for me to reach her, and the story can't be made longer. I could describe him as he walked away when we parted, round-shouldered and disorientated. When I met him he was on his way down to the cottage in order to reprove me. Apart from the postman no one else ever comes. And the postman only comes rarely because in general I prefer to have my letters sent home and not here.

I get up and walk up and down in some doubt.

SA

O nce in the car I feel like another man. Or rather, it seems to me that only now am I really myself, as though all my reveries are being left behind in the cottage.

Luckily, there won't be many people about on the roads, I have to drive fast so as not to be late. It would be too annoying to lose any time, for there isn't too much as it is. Twelve minutes, I think, if the train's on time. Alone for three quarters of an hour in each direction just so that we can be together for twelve minutes.

Luckily the weather is fair and the driving makes no demands on me. Besides, Toran Lynde's problems about putting his experiences on public display are sufficient to occupy my attention on the way. A whole life is a pretty tall order, even if it is devoid of happenings. If only you could be allowed to concentrate on arranging a shortish period at a time.

I have a race with the train for the last bit of the way. It wins, of course. Running down the steps after leaving the car under a sign saying No Parking, I see that Diam is already on the platform.

I run towards her. A living orange dot in the midst of grey surroundings. I launch myself into her fountain of beauty. Once more she is a slender figure in my arms.

'I got here first,' she whispers in my ear.

I am too out of breath to reply, but I hold her a little tighter.

'Can you use me?' she goes on.

'Always,' I say as usual, indicating with a squeeze that I will never let her go. 'Let's run away together.'

She laughs, even more happily than usual.

'No, for three days. Doria's on the train; she's going to take my place.'

'No, not on your life,' I say, holding her still more firmly. She laughs so beautifully that I try to find some way of continuing.

'Just let me go for a couple of minutes; let me explain, Alian.'

'Not on your life; do you expect me to let you loose for a sixth of the time we've got?'

I have failed to take account of the fact that the train was a couple of minutes late.

Nevertheless, she tears herself away.

'You can borrow me for three whole days. Can you use me?'

I am confused. A girl has poked her head out of the window and is staring at us.

'That's Doria,' says Diam. 'She knows all about it. She's going to go on and pretend she's me.'

'She can't,' I say.

I realize that Doria has caught my words, but she just laughs.

I can scarcely bring myself to listen while I look at Diam's beautiful lips. She slowly explains things, smiling now and then. And when the train starts she waves to Doria. And when I shout, 'But what about your suitcase?' she laughs again and says, 'Doria's going to keep that.'

It has dawned on me that Doria is going to take a hotel room in Diam's name. She, Doria, needs to be alone for a time. And she, Diam, needs to be together with me, she says. Afterwards, she'll have Doria's hotel bill to show; her husband, Diam's husband, won't be able to discover anything. The twelve minutes, which I could hardly be bothered to reach out for, have grown into three days. I have been presented with a

13

magnificent bouquet when I have been hoping for no more than a couple of seeds.

We are in the car on the way back to the cottage. I don't know how a child feels, but I think that's how I'm feeling. I have dreamt of her for years, but we have only rarely had the chance of more than a quarter of an hour together. Either Mea has been in the way, or Diam's husband. He is a big, taciturn chap whom I can hardly ever get a word out of. Diam usually tells stories of how he sometimes shadows her when she goes to town shopping.

She twirls the heart I'm wearing round my neck. She gives me a look of playful reproach.

'No, you drive,' I say. She loves to drive my car.

We change places. Although it's a small car, we can manage without getting out.

Now I have both hands free. I know of no one so ready to accept as she. She has a mole on her cheek that can only be seen from the passenger side.

When I touch it she smiles. She turns her head and looks happily at me.

During the drive she has no time to look in the mirror, so I try a couple of times to tell her how beautiful she is. I don't succeed.

I kiss her hand, and that, too, makes her smile.

Is she really as happy about this as I?

It has begun to grow light when we reach the cottage. She runs indoors and lies down, tired, on the bed.

She is so lovely that my thoughts come to a standstill.

'Oh, you're so beautiful,' I say, snuggling my head close to hers.

'Is that the only reason why I'm lying here?'

I hesitate, not knowing what to reply.

There is a bond between me and reality. It is tight and constricting. There are two ways in which I can try to reduce the inconvenience caused by it: I can change myself, or I can change my world.

I put down my ball pen and get up.

She has continued her journey now. I'm not thinking of her.

I take the pile of literary histories and start to look up in the indexes. When there is a reference to Marel or Lanson I make a note of it. Only a single work mentions both of them. I read through what it says in order to see whether the author makes any reflections on the phenomenon. But he has not noted anything. Only devotes a single line to Marel, makes no mention at all of *The Man on the Road*. G. F. Lanson receives the greater part of a page. There is a reference to *What the World Showed*, but *The Man on the Road* isn't brought into the picture.

Everything is completely silent. There is just a murmur from the sea. I have not been out for a long time, so I'll go for a walk before long.

I can't refrain from mentioning an event that is supposed to have taken place round here.

A group of people are said to have foregathered in a restaurant. The mood is supposed to have been animated, and various events must have taken place. Altogether there were presumably ten or twelve people present. Their prejudices diminished in time with the wine in their bottles.

In a moment inspiring confidences, a young and rather unprepossessing man got up and admitted that he was not participating in the party because he found it amusing, but that in the scant amount of free time he enjoyed he had begun to write a novel and he was now taking part in all kinds of conviviality in order to derive impressions from it and learn what human beings are really like.

After the young man's confession a strange atmosphere made itself felt among those present, until one of the others, a rather older and otherwise highly respected man, shocked everyone by telling them in a husky voice that in fact he was taking part in the merrymaking with exactly the same intention. Admittedly, his hack work wasn't much good, he conceded, but it gave him personally great satisfaction, and several members of his family had been enthusiastic about the way in which he could capture a rustic atmosphere, whereas his ability to describe ordinary, uncomplicated people left a good deal to be desired. And so he was participating in the merrymaking in order to learn from those taking part.

At this moment a young woman broke out in convulsive laughter – which the assembled company noted very attentively. Almost sobbing, she told them she was in almost the same situation as both the young man and the older one, though her intention was to compose some caustic poems to expose the ridiculous, desperate urge for entertainment that was spreading like wildfire through all levels of the population. She was not the least ashamed to admit that her role in the party was that of a spy, for she believed it to be her moral duty to issue a fierce warning against this tendency, and so she was compelled to acquaint herself with the phenomenon.

After this woman's contribution there were three or four participants ready to make their confessions: one was going to write a book about everyday life in this parish, another was writing a drama on the class struggle, one was publishing brief humorous portraits in the form of short stories, and one was fantasising about a gigantic epic to illustrate the fate of mankind.

Before the hour had elapsed, all the revellers had made their confession. Every one of them had been present in order to deepen their insight into human conduct so as subsequently to be able to put it into print, whether in the form of a detective novel or a beautiful four-lined stanza.

The participants are said to have bought a farm out on the moors and all to have moved out there. Thereafter they lived together and all described their lives to the extent of their individual abilities.

When they were all dead it is said that a bonfire which burned for four days was made of the heaps of written papers discovered in the place.

This reminds me of too much. I search in front of me and find some pages written in the same hand as that of the present writer. In them I read an account of a man who is made unhappy at being presented with his story.

What is written on the other sheets is very reminiscent of what I have just written here. With some justification I could maintain that whoever was the source of one set of notes is also the source of the other. And call this source myself.

I feel this is right. And feel at the same time that in some way I have cut something out – as though at the same time I am continuing my dreams somewhere else.

Moreover, my resolution implies something else: that something has happened. Time has passed. I am writing one set of notes; the other is already finished.

My heart is pounding against the edge of the table as I get up to ponder this new situation.

SAL

H er question causes me quite a few problems. We have gone down to the beach to watch the daybreak. It's too much to hope the sun will rise, too. We have lain down in the shelter of a boat that has been dragged up on the beach.

We kiss now and then, sometimes pretty passionately. Our fingers play with each other as we expect them to do. I wonder how deep into my soul I must reach to find an acceptable answer.

I needn't tell her that I am terribly fond of her, and that I have watched her admiringly for years. Besides, she knows as well as I that there can never be any permanent relationship between us with the two spouses standing in our way, and knowing that we each feel bound to them.

Nevertheless, I begin with: 'I'm terribly fond of you. I think of you almost all the time. So I derive a great deal of joy from you, even if we can't be together very much.'

'You ought to let me take part in your joys,' she says, again turning over the heart so that the D appears.

She becomes more serious and says, 'But then it's not easy when such a long time elapses without our seeing each other. Don't you agree?'

'Yes, but I'm happy to be in touch with you even if it does lead to problems. Perhaps even *because* it leads to problems. Perhaps I'm deliberately launching myself into the biggest emotional difficulties I can find. I mean, going and doing something so foolish as to fall in love with a woman I can't hope to win, and trying to live with her now for a couple of days so that I can fully appreciate what I am missing every day.

Perhaps I'm doing this so as to be able to describe it afterwards, so as to become the omni-suffering author?'

'I don't believe you,' she says.

'At any rate, I have a feeling that I can write better after meeting you, after being faced with a host of problems because of you. Until now I've almost had the impression that I'd resolved all my difficulties and got rid of them. But I must admit I've got something to write about now.'

I smile in an effort to trivialize my words.

Meanwhile, our hands have become very preoccupied with each other. We make an unsuccessful effort to get closer to each other. We decide to go back to the warmth of the cottage.

We put more wood on the fire and place a rug in front of it. Quite slowly, we undress each other. I admire every conquest I make, enjoy her all the more because it is so long since I last saw her.

We lie down close together on the rug. I find it hard to get an erection. Only when the fire starts to burn more brightly and I become aware of the shadow her body casts on the blue curtain, does it help. I refrain from telling her about my little problem for the third time: the first couple of times I'm together with a girl I'm so self-conscious that I can't carry out my intentions, and after that she'll be so disappointed with me that there will never be a third time. I know that Diam no longer finds the story interesting.

We creep tight close to each other.

I caress her slender body, find it difficult to get away from the thought of how unusual this situation is. So preoccupied am I with this that I have a sense of standing beside us, looking at my body intertwined with hers. Seeing her leg sliding up and down mine. When, in the midst of a kiss, I look into her eye I realize that she has the same feeling, she, too, is standing beside us looking at our bodies as we make love. Standing there, we cannot remain unaffected by this sight, my hand slides across to the girl at my side, coming to rest on her thigh, moving down it and up it.

She responds to my caresses, and we turn towards each other and slide into each other.

We remain lying beside each other for a long time. We fall asleep, waken up and find we are cold, with some difficulty we get hold of a couple of extra blankets without parting, and immediately fall asleep again.

SAN

'You're lying here because I love you,' I say at last.
'What do you mean by that?' she teases. 'What about Mea?'

'I mean that I am going to make these three days my whole life,' I reply on a sudden impulse.

'Here, a life in a cottage, surely that's not what you're going to offer me? Miles away from everything.'

'No, come on, we'll go off into the world, we'll go off and live life.'

I have leapt up. Her voice puzzles me so much that I don't always know what to say.

'You don't mean that,' she says, sitting down. She shakes her hair so it falls into place. 'You're not like that at all.'

'No, you're right. So let's do it for that very reason.'

Now, I obviously do mean it. I even feel quite keen. Once more, I have transformed myself into another person.

Another five minutes and we are once more in the car, bumping along the uneven track. Now it is me driving.

She fiddles with the heart hanging round my neck.

'If you meant anything with all this,' she murmurs close to my ear. 'Then you'd fix this thing so the side with me on is always showing.'

'No, sometimes your side deserves to be closest to my heart.'

She switches on the car radio. It emits a languorous melody played on a tenor sax.

'How would you like me when we get to the hotel?' she asks cheerfully.

She holds up her hair and looks like a tight-lipped, but

21

beautiful, colonel's wife. She wraps her scarf around her head, draws up her collar, and looks like some angelic nun.

'Or would you rather have a witch?' she says, making an effort to look menacing.

While I'm convincing her that she is the sweetest witch I have ever met, we get so close to the side of the road that I have to stop.

'You're mine for three days,' I comment thoughtfully between two kisses.

She looks at me in surprise: 'Oh, so that's what you think?'

It is already morning when we reach the town. Of course there are no parking spaces anywhere near the hotel we have decided on.

She jumps out, goes into the hotel to reserve a room, and is welcomed by an admiring hall porter. I drive on to get rid of the car.

When, at last, I find a parking space, I realize that in all decency we must have some luggage with us. I hurry to buy a suitcase and a few things to throw into it, and when I've managed to find the hotel again I act as though it's so heavy that my back is breaking under the strain of carrying it.

Diam is not in the lobby. She must have gone up to our room. I ask the porter to show me where I can find the lady who has just arrived. He looks at me indignantly, and explains that this is contrary to the rules. He is only allowed to show the way to the men who are staying in the rooms.

I am most graciously allowed to take a look at the register of guests. According to the list, three couples have arrived on this particular day. I don't know which of them is me. All the names are in the porter's handwriting.

I make a quick decision. Diam has not made my choice easy. She has made either a pastor, a colonel or a director of me.

I slip out, run round the corner, and in a department store there I buy a distinguished-looking military cap. I stuff my hair up into it, smooth my moustache and march proudly into the hotel.

'I am Colonel Gahl,' I say in my most stentorian voice. 'Would you please show me up to my room?'

The porter gives me a sceptical look. I glance around absent-mindedly, slapping myself noisily and rhythmically on the thigh with my right hand.

He shows me right up to the door. He knocks and says respectfully, 'The colonel has arrived, madam.'

An august voice virtually sings out to me: 'Splendid, do come in, beloved.'

The porter pushes me maliciously into the lioness's embrace. I am received with surprising kindness. It takes me the better part of two minutes to wriggle out of the embrace while eagerly explaining something to the effect that this is an unfortunate misunderstanding. The lady seems reluctant to consider the misunderstanding as unfortunate, but finally I manage to extricate myself.

I run down the corridor and slip out through a back door.

It would be like Diam to have made a pastor of me. I stuff the cap into my case. At a newspaper stand I buy a paperback with a black cover. I turn my jacket collar up a little more and go back to the hotel.

The porter gives me a dubious look as I unconcernedly stride across to the counter.

'I am Pastor Tromin. Would you please be so kind as to show me to my room.'

I make sure to keep my hand over the letters revealing that the book is entitled Alpha One.

The porter mutters something under his breath and leads me to Mrs. Tromin's door.

'Mrs. Tromin, your husband is here,' he says in a rather peculiar tone.

'Oh dear,' replies a submissive voice from inside. 'Just a moment, I'm coming.'

There are sounds of hurried activity behind the door, a chair is overturned, a cupboard opened and closed twice, and meanwhile the porter fixes me with his disgusting eyes.

'Do come in, dear,' the unknown voice says at last. 'I looked terrible, I didn't want you to see me like that.'

The door has opened. The lady, who has obviously not finished her personal toilet, has her back to me and is busy in front of the mirror. The door closes silently behind me.

'I'm so sorry, madam. I had to put on this act in order to get in touch with you.'

She looks at me as though she were seeing sights.

'Who are you?' she gasps.

'I am a vision,' I reply. 'We have started using more up-to-date methods.'

'Get out, or I'll call my husband,' she shrieks.

'With pleasure. If you refuse this offer, it's your own fault,' I reply in a meaningful voice.

And then I quickly withdraw.

When I reappear in the lobby again the porter only discovers me when I breathe a cloud of smoke from my cigar into his face. But the effort only makes me cough myself.

'I am Mr. Levon, the company director,' I murmur, scattering a few coins on the counter. 'My room.'

The porter suddenly seems to wake up when he catches sight of the banknote sticking out of my pocket.

I have a feeling that he makes a long detour on the way to my room, like a zealous taxi driver expecting to be paid in relation to the distance driven.

He knocks on the door.

'Excuse me, Miss,' he says, with a cruel smile. 'Your husband's here.'

STO

If my hypothesis is correct, I have to think of myself as a chain of beings creating themselves by writing. In the same way as I am doing now, in the same way as did he who told about the man refusing to acknowledge his own story, and in the same way as did he giving the account of the writers' party. I have called them S and ST the more easily to maintain my overall view.

I push the paper a little to one side and get up.

Standing there beside the writing desk I suddenly realize that I still lack an important element in my argument.

I have been able to determine this connection thanks to the fact that in my S-self and my ST-self I committed myself to writing. But just as a moment ago I was standing beside the writing desk without writing, there may well be many other versions of me that will never be written down.

The sea is fairly rough tonight. I have an urge to go down and watch it, but before I do I must conclude this train of thought.

Just as S is not necessarily only followed by ST; one could well imagine an unformulated SA, SB and SC. Similarly, my present self, STO is not the only possible continuation of ST. I might have brothers, STA, STB whom I can't see, but only imagine.

And so I must also envisage the possibility that something might rub off not only from one link to those following it, from ST till STA and STB, but also between 'neighbours', between links ranged side by side and stemming from the same predecessor, that is to say between STA, STB and STC. So that I have to see my STO-self linked to potentials of which I have only been dimly aware, but which are unfolding themselves outside me, or somewhere else within me.

Is that why it feels as though the sea is attracting me? Is that why thoughts of her force themselves on me, as though a dream film is being played in my head without my being able to take it in?

So when I do something that surprises me, does it stem from an experience that one of my kindred potentials has just had?

I feel that I have caught hold of one end of a pattern, without having the slightest idea of what I might find at the other end, and without knowing a method for uncovering the rest of it.

A local man is said to have suffered an unusual fate; I can't resist recounting the event, as I think it is connected with my study.

The man disappeared some time ago. An immediate search is organized. A number of people who have been together with him are found in the capital. But moreover, a family living near the border, that is to say at the opposite end of the country, make it known that they were having a visit from him at exactly the same time.

In a restaurant in the capital he has told a friend he has come across by chance that he has been involved in a road accident and has since been drifting around with no real recollection of what has happened. The friend wants to put him in touch with the police or his family, but the man refuses, fearing that he has committed some punishable offence and wanting to find out for himself what he has done in the time that has elapsed.

He has given more or less the same explanation to a business acquaintance he has looked up in order to get hold of some money. This person has thought the man was merely having him on.

But at exactly the same time, the man has been visiting a family he knows at the other end of the country, and there he has told them that he has left his wife and intends going somewhere far away to start all over again.

The search for the man continued, without his ever being found or rather without either of him ever being found. However, occasionally they came across people who had been together with one or the other edition of him.

It is still a strange thought to me that I am here in the midst of a net, with versions of myself on both sides of me and versions of myself in front and behind, versions about which I have previously only had the vaguest notion, and with which I still only have a very limited contact.

It strikes me that I can hereby send a greeting to that version of me that is following me.

Everything is still obscure to me. I can perceive more and more ways of proceeding, without knowing which of them will guide me to my goal.

STR

T he first thing I do is convince myself that there is not too much life in the fireplace. I leave some of the lights on so as to be able to find my way back more easily, lock the cottage and go out into the night.

I have been rather alarmed to find these sheets of paper attesting that I have written away yet another day. I feel as though I have lived each of my days separately, without attempting to establish any relationship between them. Every morning I have started over again on a new day, so that my days are scattered around me haphazardly, just as they have turned up out of the blue. I have only been able to see quite a short way into the future and so have tried to give each day its own story.

I decide that my perception of this relationship must furnish me with an opportunity to direct my life, to fashion my own story.

As I walk down to the beach, it is as though someone bumps into me. I look round in surprise, but of course there is no one within sight.

The waves are not terribly high, I am walking right out by the water's edge, where the sand is firm. I keep up a good pace while trying to think through the new situation in which I find myself. Despite my profession, I have only rarely thought of myself as the author of my own life, as bearing sole responsibility for the story that emerges from it. And on previous occasions when the thought has struck me, I have dismissed it as a romantic fancy, and not sought to understand its implications.

My walk has taken me pretty far away from home. I have

reached a place where there is a row of big posts. Even from a distance I have a feeling that someone is sitting on one of these posts, but I have to get considerably closer before I am completely sure.

It is so unusual to meet anyone on the beach at this time of night that I direct my steps past the man to see if he needs help.

'Good evening,' I say. 'Is there anything wrong?'

'Yes, you could say that, I suppose,' he replies with a melancholy smile that indicates to me that things are not entirely hopeless.

He's a weird man. As he doesn't get up, I can't make out whether he is tall or short; his face is round, with a large number of wrinkles that make a strange, alien impression. His eyes are almost closed by wrinkles.

'We must both be out on the same errand,' I say, and again he smiles.

He offers a post to me. I sit down and in a few sentences tell him something of my problem.

'I well understand you,' he says. 'We need to experience more, that's what's the matter. The mature person has only one real experience to look forward to: death; and that's not particularly enlivening, is it?'

His pessimism appears to be greater than mine, so I risk a mild objection: 'Oh, surely you can always think of something?'

'But the real experiences are all behind us,' he persists. 'We have fought the battle represented by growing up, developing from being nothing to being an individual, the merciless, bloody, exciting, exhausting experience of creating an identity.'

I would have protested at this point if he hadn't got so well into his stride.

'And we've tried that experience glorified in almost all our stories, films and songs and so on as *the* experience: the experience of searching for the other person, finding her and growing together with her. Well, I assume you are married, too.'

I nod, although I don't expect he can see me.

'Finally, as a grown man, we've experienced having children, setting in motion a recurrence of ourselves, duplicating ourselves. After the process of growing up, love and procreation there is nothing really new for ordinary people, no real experiences in prospect until, many years hence, the dissolution of identity takes place.'

Suddenly we hear a loud shout, apparently coming from the sea.

'What was that?' I exclaim, leaping down from my post.

'It sounded as though someone was surrendering his identity,' he replies carelessly. 'Or perhaps it was the starting signal for a new one.'

'But didn't it come from out at sea?'

'Oh, yes. But you shouldn't bother about that, we experience so many things.'

Again I sit down on the top of a post.

'What do we do in the long period between procreation and death?' I say in order to bring him back to his train of thought.

'We resort to pseudo-experiences. We try to live on the basis of other people's experiences: the children's growing up, their love and procreation. We wallow in surrogate experiences: literature, television, films, magazines that make us re-experience our great love. We exploit people who reject the normal pattern, we worship idols, try to live on the experiences of others.'

Slowly, he turns his head, as though he has already a hundred times seen what his eyes alight on.

'What we need,' he concludes as he jumps down elegantly from his post. 'What we need is a philosopher who can reinterpret our lives, who can give us an understanding capable of making our later years just as rich in experience as life's beginning. As things stand now, the share-out is appallingly unequal.'

I can think of nothing with which to comment on this view of his. We take leave of each other, he walks away from the beach, I turn round and start to go back the way I came.

I have not gone far before reaching a house from which music and light are streaming. A man approaches me, he has a bottle in his hand.

SALA

When I wake up, I feel empty. I have to make an effort to find a suitable way of continuing. She is lying awake by my side.

'I'm glad I've got you to make me feel miserable,' I say, kissing her where she is most beautiful. She blushes, and smiles, still more or less asleep.

'Your compliments are somewhat ambiguous,' she says.

'The intention was good, at any rate.'

I am about to launch into a lengthy explanation of how I think it better to be tormented with gloom, to suffer the pangs of expectation so as perhaps to fulfil some hope for a brief moment, rather than to end in a state of diminished sensitivity in which one's problems admittedly are overcome. But before even starting, I realize that it is an elementary mistake to repeat yourself.

'I'm engaged on a great project,' I say eagerly. 'I'm going to write a vast guide to How to Become Unhappy.'

She smiles in disbelief. I realize that I shall have to go into more detail.

'Essentially, it will consist of four major parts. The third of them will be about you and be concerned with setting oneself unattainable objectives and making demands that cannot be fulfilled.'

'Thank you, how flattering,' she says, moving her lips in the direction of mine. Suddenly she draws back again. 'But you did fulfil my demands just now.'

My disappointed lips form the words: 'The motto of the book is to be: No day is lived without pain or without a hope that failed. And, incidentally, it wasn't just now: we've been asleep almost all day.'

'I must go into town and buy some clothes, so I can have a hope of disappointing you yet again. Doria took my suitcase with her, you know.'

'If you think you can look more beautiful,' I begin.

'No,' she interrupts, 'But different.'

It is quite difficult to drive along an uneven gravel road while the most beautiful woman in the world is sitting beside you slowly and painstakingly putting on her clothes, from the most intimate to the most visible.

The town receives us with open arms, even though Diam has long been respectably dressed.

She doesn't allow herself the time to be guided by her famous intuition, but makes straight for the first shop she comes across. I follow in her wake, gathering up all the admiring looks that go her way, but which she simply doesn't have time to harvest.

For once it's a delight to go shopping. I saunter along behind her as though it were I who owned her, and see how excited she becomes when she finds something that is likely to suit her. She turns around with a short nightdress that she provocatively holds up in front of her, awakening a host of shameless thoughts.

'Would you be terribly disappointed if I bought it?'

There is no need for me to answer; my eyes have already given me away. With my ever wider open eyes as a yardstick she makes a triumphant round from shop to shop. I don't know how she contrives to buy a toothbrush with dignity, stockings with charm and nail-polisher with elegance, but when she has finished I have a feeling that at no time has she touched the earth with an entire foot. Finally, when the back seat of the car can't take any more, she buys a little block of chocolate.

'For you,' she says in a sugary tone. 'If there is room for it in the car.'

We drive all over town to find a place that can tempt us. The only one we find is a restaurant with 'cabaret every evening'.

We glance sceptically at each other.

SALM

On awakening, I feel empty. Diam is wakening up, too.
'What now?' I happen to say.

I have a strange feeling that we no longer have any use for each other. In a way things were easier when she was beautiful and out of reach. Now she is simply rather lovely to look at. I give her a kiss.

I suspect she has the same feeling, of having started a game that simply can't go on for three days.

'Will you drive me into town?' she says. 'I need to do some shopping.'

We hardly speak on the way.

When we separate, she says, 'I shall have to go and visit some friends. It's an arrangement I made some time ago. My husband might possibly ring them, so I shall have to be there. You don't mind, do you? Will you pick me up here tomorrow morning? We've still got two days left.'

I hasten to show how well I understand. I can't make up my mind whether she is making a fool of me, or whether to believe her explanation. In one way it suits me quite well to be left on my own again for a while.

She kisses me and looks so happily at me as she goes off that I am convinced that she really has arranged to see her friends.

I drive for a while and find a restaurant that of course is overcrowded. I am given a seat at a table where another man is already sitting.

I offer him a drink, but with exaggerated courtesy he refuses, adding a long explanation to the effect that he used to drink a great deal, but that when he realized that this reduced his potential, he stopped.

I only half listen to his moralizing, and from a desire to show him that I don't feel stung by his words I immediately order myself two glasses. I realize at once how childish my action must seem, and when, soon afterwards, a rather hefty blonde comes along and sits at our table, I nonchalantly push one of the glasses across to her.

The table looks as though it has been standing on the same spot since the Stone Age. If not, then it's a good imitation.

Up by the bar, which by way of contrast is made of plastic so as to satisfy every taste, there is a very self-assured young man. The girl he is together with has large breasts, but is otherwise not particularly striking.

'We're only playing roles,' exclaims the young man, to the accompaniment of a grandiose gesture that could make any Hamlet blush with shame. Perhaps he has just been reading a book.

'Rubbish,' says the girl. ' 'Cause my feelings for you are not merely a role play. When I say I love you, I mean it.'

Well, she's not quite right in this; she looks as though she is profoundly fed up with her boyfriend's urge to shine on the basis of some half-digested superior knowledge.

'No, that's a role, too,' he exclaims.

I try to find a more interesting object for my attention. The blonde looks pretty eager, so I avoid looking in her direction.

There's a sweet young couple there, obviously out together for the first time. The girl has a large suitcase that they have dragged right into the restaurant. Moreover, she is very good-looking; in ten years she will be a real beauty. I look at my watch and decide that I haven't time to wait for her.

'Could you perhaps act as though you weren't keen on me?' asks the girl at the bar, in a voice so penetrating that my attention is caught once more.

'No problem,' replies he with the superior knowledge, giving her a peck on the cheek. 'You just watch.'

At last, my order arrives.

The self-assured chap has completely changed his manner. His tokens of attention to the girl have gone; he drinks more than before and appears to be concentrating on his glass. The girl sits there, strangely superfluous, observing his distant manner.

I feel tempted to get up and applaud his role play, but at the moment I am not the sort to behave like that.

The man's eyes wander around the room and finally stop at the resplendent blonde at my side. They come to rest so heavily on this table companion of mine that I can almost hear her being crushed beneath their weight. With his lips half open, he smiles in this direction. I don't return the smile – it's presumably not me he is trying to seduce.

His girl obviously feels uncomfortable at his changed manner; she gets up to go to the toilet. I am waiting for my dessert in any case, so I get up and follow her.

She is tidying her hair in front of the mirror in the foyer. I try to strike up a conversation with her; she doesn't exactly brush me off, but at least she's pretty surly. So I give up trying to force my attentions on her and return to my table without any further ado.

Her friend has gone. As she comes in again, a waiter immediately goes across to her and gives her a message from the vanished boyfriend; he will ring and explain it all tomorrow. My blond table companion has disappeared, too.

Scarcely have I started on my dessert when a woman enters. She is in some sexless uniform, and seems curiously robust and out of place in these surroundings.

Suddenly, she starts addressing all the guests in a loud voice. A complete silence falls in the room. She tells us that alcohol will be the ruination of us, it estranges us from life and true love.

A waiter pushes his way across to her and makes to show her out, but a drunken man in the other end of the room protests.

'We want to hear the truth,' he shouts. 'Give her a glass from me instead.'

The girl at the bar smiles wryly at this intermezzo. The waiter gives up.

The woman in uniform continues: 'We are here to love one another, and we can't do that when we have filled ourselves with alcohol.'

At this juncture I get up and kiss her cheek. She blushes more deeply than they do even in novels nowadays, turns on her heels and disappears with a half-smothered sound in her throat.

The girl with the wry smile gets up and leaves. I leave a banknote for the waiter and am only slightly irritated with myself for tipping him too much. I go after her.

This time she condescends to exchange a few words with me. And to my amazement, when I suggest taking her along to another bar, she says yes.

Actually, I have only intended chatting with her for a short while, but the loneliness we have in common takes us from the bar back to her hotel room.

Here we play an unusual game. We kiss a couple of times, without feeling that this will stop the world for either of us. After a few more caresses, we both go to bed, but not with each other. We simply each go to our own bed, and exchange a few more caresses. It is obvious that we both feel that if we went on, it would not be because of any natural urge, but simply represent an attempt to avenge our way out of our loneliness.

Actually, it's quite stimulating to settle down and sleep beside an unknown, naked woman without first having taken her, so stimulating that at one time I find it difficult to adhere to our unspoken chaste resolution. Not least disturbing is the fact that after falling asleep she accidentally comes to lie with her backside sticking out from under the duvet only a hand's breadth away from me.

The following morning the telephone rings; I am the first awake, and I take it quite automatically. It's her boyfriend. She creeps over to me, in my bed; she feels strangely smooth and unused against my bare skin. Together we listen to the boyfriend's explanation. She really must forgive him, but he fell for a girl yesterday evening, he stammers, of course, he hopes she'll take it nicely. At first he started making approaches to the other woman just for fun, but the role had suited him so well that he decided to go on playing it.

The loss doesn't seem to affect her too badly. She smiles her wry smile and puts the receiver down. As I am leaving, the telephone rings again.

I arrive in time to collect Diam. We both seem to be well rested and chat enthusiastically to each other on the way back to the cottage. Nevertheless, it is as though some feeling of discontent is churning within me; I don't know what I can do to get rid of it.

SAND

Diam gives me an inquisitive look as I enter.

'What a mess you look! You're so untidy. Do you *have* to behave like a teenager, just because you're away for a couple of days?' she drones.

With a gracious gesture she motions the porter to go.

I tidy my clothes a little. I know two things about this director called Levon, the man I am to be now: I must have plenty of money, and I must have good taste. The woman standing in front of me, who is supposed to be my wife, is ample evidence of both. I honestly feel a little uncertain about how to play the part expected of me.

'Rotten cigar,' I mumble irritably, throwing it down. Well, at least that was one problem I had got rid of.

'Will you ring down to Reception and ask them to arrange the beds separately,' continues my august wife.

'Listen, don't you think we ought to find another game to play? I feel such a bloody fool in this one.'

'Where on earth do you get these slang expressions from? What "game" are you talking about?'

I sit down on the bed. I have run up and down the stairs so much that I am bathed in sweat. But I feel almost too embarrassed to take off my shirt and wash in full view of the Director's wife.

'I shall have to leave you for a while, I have an appointment to keep,' I say in a moment of inspiration. 'It may be that one of my friends will turn up, an author, quite a lad, but you'll look after him, won't you?'

I make to give her a kiss on the cheek before going, but don't even manage that.

'Visitors at this hour? I thought we were going out. Honestly, why did you bring me along? Do you think you can order me about as though I was one of your employees?'

She is still speaking when I emerge into the corridor. Once more I tidy my clothes. I knock on Diam's door and go in before she has a chance to answer.

'I am sorry, madam. I thought I would find Mr. Levon here. My name is Sandme. I have arranged to see Mr. Levon. Perhaps you wouldn't mind if I wait?'

This time it is Diam who doesn't know what to do. I have taken a seat before she has managed to gather her wits. You have to be quick to do that.

'No, please do take a seat,' she says sardonically.

Completely unruffled, she continues her toilette. She must have enormous resources in that little handbag of hers.

I become somewhat peevish at first. I get up and wander about a little. Her disapproving glance is so discrete that I would not normally have noticed anything. I move quite close to her.

'What a lovely necklace you have there,' I say, placing a cautious hand on her neck.

'Thank you,' she says, getting up. 'I think my husband will be here any moment now. Wouldn't you like to wait? I'm afraid shall have to leave you.'

It really does seem that she's going to go out. She has reached the door before I manage to throw myself at her, clasping her beautiful legs.

'Forgive me,' I say in desperation. 'I don't know what I'm doing. I have loved you ever since I set eyes on you. I can't resist any longer.'

'Will you please let go immediately. I shall have to ring for the porter.'

'Oh, stop it, Diam. I can't be bothered any more. I give

up.'

I have got up. I can't help being a little bit peeved.

'Do stop this nonsense. Accept that you know me, and let's go out and have something to eat. You've brought it off quite well, I admit, but . .'

She makes to go, still maintaining the mien of a director's wife. I grab hold of her and draw her reluctant body towards me and kiss her. She does not struggle violently to escape, but yet so much that I let go of her.

At that moment the porter arrives. I don't know when she has rung for him.

'Would you please show this gentleman out,' she says in a charming voice. 'I'm afraid he can't wait until my husband returns.'

The porter takes me by the scruff of the neck. I struggle free, but go with him. He makes sure that I am right out on the pavement before going inside again. He places himself with arms crossed and with a vacant expression, pretending not to notice that I am standing outside the window with arms crossed, sticking out my tongue at him.

SANG

Diam winks at me as I enter.

'Did you have difficulty in finding me?' she asks, when the porter has disappeared, shaking his head.

I tell her of my little contretemps with the porter, overdo it a bit and entangle myself in a complete farce.

Diam laughs delightfully.

'What plans have you got now?'

Something compels me to go over and put my arms round her. I kiss her neck, her cheek, her forehead. She accepts this in such a way that there is no stopping.

'If we're to go out for a meal, it must be somewhere where you only need to use one hand to eat with,' she says.

We drive to a Japanese restaurant.

'I have so much been looking forward to these three days,' she says.

Her voice is at once a little nervous and very happy.

'I've been looking forward to it far more than you have.'

'You're a bad liar. You couldn't even be certain I'd be able to stay with you.'

'But I could presumably look forward to it, all the same.'

'I was afraid you wouldn't come to meet the train. You know, you had said that those ten minutes were hardly worth ...'

'I nearly didn't come, either. But I went on picturing you to myself. And then I thought that seeing the original would be far better than leafing through my memories.'

In the restaurant we are suitably amused at how bad we are with chopsticks. Again and again I praise my good fortune in having a hand free to move about over her and make it even more difficult for her to eat. We have found a corner in the restaurant where no one can see us.

She feels so young and responsive to my touch, like a flower unfolding beneath my caresses. I have an urge to make some contribution to repay all the beauty emanating from her.

My silence makes my throat burn, and yet I can't think of anything to say.

Suddenly I come to think of a couple of characters from a novel, call to mind their eloquent manner of speaking, and seek to emulate them.

'Shall I tell you about an adventure I've had?'

'Yes please,' she replies, seemingly pleasantly surprised.

'Or perhaps I really ought to say I've dreamt it. No, it's a lot of rubbish, really.'

'You'll not get a kiss until you've told it to me. What was it you were going to say?'

There is no way out.

'I must have dreamt it, for it was a world where you could simply exchange parts of your body if you wanted. And you can't do that here, can you? For instance, I'm not all that keen on my ears – you can see they stick out rather. But incidentally, they used to be even worse. So when I met a man with nicer ears, I suggested doing a swap with him, and strangely enough, he said yes. Perhaps he'd been dreaming longingly of having ears that stick out. We did a swap. And that was that.'

'How nice,' she says.

She doesn't seem to be disappointed, so I risk going on.

'That's not all. Soon after that I met a man who had fallen in love with my nose, and as his wasn't noticeably ugly, I agreed to a swap when he suggested it. On another occasion I came across a pair of legs that were longer than mine, and I arranged an exchange. In this way I gradually managed to trade quite a lot of new parts for my body. But incidentally, I soon became tired of my new nose, and managed to exchange it for a rather retroussé one that I thought was quite fun.'

I show her my current nose, which naturally can't stand comparison with hers, but which she is so kind as to kiss.

'Now, my dream changes character. I am on a visit to a young lady, a blonde, who is awfully impressed to be talking to an author. She tells me she's expecting a friend who would like to meet me. He has been very taken with a couple of my books, including a story in which I invented the subsequently famous phrase: of course, you can't be in two places at the same time. This admirer has become a passionate collector, explains the blond lady. She is interrupted by the arrival of the person she's been expecting. I get up and suddenly stand motionless. For a moment I feel as though I'm standing in front of a mirror, but then I realize what is happening. A hand that used to be mine is stretched out to me, and lips that once were mine speak to me – as far as I can hear, it is even my own original vocal chords saying: "I've so much been looking forward to meeting you. You don't know me, but I've been collecting all the parts of your body for the past couple of years."'

Diam laughs so loudly that a little Japanese waitress comes running. We put on innocent expressions. The waitress goes away when she is convinced that there is no one hiding in the other corners.

'Have you really changed so much?' asks Diam teasingly. 'Isn't there the least little bit left of the old Alian?'

'What about going back to the hotel to see if we can find something?'

STOL

I have now spent a great deal of time exploring the theory advanced by the predecessor of mine calling himself STO. I have managed not only to find conclusive evidence that his theory is sound, but also to define the specific conditions under which segregation takes place, and I have found the reason for it.

I would like to express my thanks for the greeting sent by my forerunner. I could naturally pass it on as a sort of chain letter, but the sender, that is to say I myself, will never be able to receive any reply, for which reason this would be a somewhat pointless procedure.

I only have a couple of days left before I am expected home from the cottage. I want to proceed as far as is humanly possible with my study. No longer do I even take time for my beloved walks along the beach, though if I took, for instance, a twenty minute walk each time I have worked for four hours it would perhaps help extricate me from the slightly over-excited condition in which I find myself. I will return to this possibility later. At the moment I feel so fully occupied that I can scarcely see my way through all that I am planning.

People have for some time been aware that our surroundings can produce those unusual mental conditions known as schizophrenia or split personality. There has been particular interest in the incidence of the condition resulting from the negative effect of one's surroundings.

Of course, we cannot rule out the possibility that a violent father, an unsympathetic mother, and so on, can be responsible for the onset of this illness. But what about those of us who feel ourselves badly treated, not by our families, but by the world?

If you expose someone to a constant threat of being killed, is it not to be expected that this person will react by going mad or suffering from paranoia? But what, then, about all of us human beings who are condemned to death, and for an unspecified period at that? Is it so surprising that we go out of our minds?

Another example: If, before a volunteer taking part in some experiment, you placed the prospect of a host of attractive, delightful and mouth-watering possibilities, and then prevented him from savouring them, and if you constantly repeated this experiment over a number of years, could you expect such a person to remain normal? But then, is this not the way in which the world treats us?

Is any other reaction than madness conceivable when we consider the boundless ocean of possibilities that we constantly see eluding us, not because others get in our way, but simply because our lives, our strength, our urges are so hugely circumscribed?

This was how the situation was before segregation became feasible. Everyone was inevitably on the verge of madness, of a personality split, resulting from the unrelenting threat of death, and the straitjacket limiting our freedom of action. Only when someone got the idea of bringing about real material segregation was the problem overcome. Even if not all the possibilities are yet at our disposal, at least they are now many times greater than they were. And the phenomenon of 'death' has completely changed character when the 'I' dying is only one link in a vast chain of selves.

The circumstances which made this possible for us deserve to be recorded.

The undertaking is thought to have been started by a certain Olvin Quer who refused to be content with living one single life. He had a family he was fond of, with which he felt comfortable and which he couldn't imagine leaving. (It has not been ascertained whether he had two or three children.) At the same time he felt powerfully attracted to a woman who, of course, was not his wife. He was what is called 'obsessed' with her and whatever the cost would not deny himself a life together with her.

This man Quer entered into some kind of collaboration with a scientist by the name of Carn Sinistre. Carn Sinistre was extremely clever and had a promising career before him; everyone expected outstanding results from him. But unfortunately for him he was strongly drawn to art and felt an overwhelming need to express himself through the medium of literature. This was his tragedy, as his scientific career did not permit him to cultivate literature with the necessary intensity. And if, instead, he devoted himself to those fanciful books he would not at the same time be able to fulfil his urge to pursue scientific research.

After encountering a great deal of opposition, these two men with their deeply divided personalities together launched the project, the project that after a long period of research and imaginative writing resulted in the first successful examples of segregation.

STOR

I think I have found the right way.

It is obvious to me now that just as I create myself in every action I undertake, so I must try to recreate myself fictionally in order to acquire the perspective, the insight to which I aspire.

At first sight my life is made up of a disorganized and chaotic conglomeration of experiences, reflections, dreams and so on, in which it is not immediately possible to see any cohesion.

Occasionally, one comes across the expression: the novel of my life. I even have a suspicion that I tend to use it myself. However, I have now realized that my life is not fashioned like a novel, when read chronologically it will not be of any aesthetic value, it is too complicated for that. But various interesting stories can be extracted from the pages of my life. And for that reason it would be better to use an expression such as my life's collection of short stories. But we are talking of a very special collection in which the individual stories are woven into each other, impinge on each other and contradict each other in the most sophisticated and tortuous ways.

In order to make possible a general view, I have furnished the few sheets I have so far accumulated with various designations in the form of capital letters. By means of these it is possible out of my chaotic experiences to extract a series of events which with a little good will can be regarded as a completed story.

Thus the final section of each story will have six letters, for instance SALMIE. (The letters are chosen so that the different variants are relatively easy to keep apart. I have not aimed at making these letters 'mean' anything.) The story ending with the section designated as SALMIE can be read in its entirety by first reading section S, then SA, then SAL, then SALM, then SALMI, after which the section designated SALMIE will provide the conclusion of the story. So you spell your way through towards the end.

You can choose your path in many different ways. When you have read S, which in this case is the beginning of all things, you can spin a coin to decide which way to go. If it shows heads you take the first continuation, SA; if it shows tails you can move to the other, ST. And by tossing a coin five times in this way you can reach the final part of the 'short story'. Thus you will reach the aforementioned SALMIE if you throw heads at the first two tries, then tails for the next two and heads for the last.

But now I will give a brief set of instructions for those individuals who are not minded to submit themselves to the vagaries of chance.

Readers who like a straightforward love story will, it is to be hoped, derive pleasure from the stories beginning with the letters SAN. Of these, SANDAT is an example of a light-hearted story, while SANGEN is just a little melancholy.

The stories beginning with STRE, too, are about the main character's encounter with a young woman, although this encounter has a rather more complex background than the SAN variations. For instance STREGL is a bitter story taken from reality. Those beginning with STRI will seem less realistic. As will be seen in the curious STRIDE episode, they are distinguished by mystery and obscurity.

The 'twin' stories SALMER and SALMET have something essential to say about people's ability to be together.

After some of the more immediately comprehensible stories have been read, some explanation of the real intention might

51

be necessary. This will be found in each of the variations beginning with STOR. A rather more contrived explanation will be found in the STOL variants.

However, the wisest course you could take first of all would perhaps be to read the SALAMO story (need I repeat? S-SA-SAL-SALA-SALAM-SALAMO), from which you will discover that in all circumstances in this life it is important to choose your path for yourself.

STRE

I t's quite obvious he wants to speak to me. I go to meet him, although I feel a little hesitant.

'Hi, comrade. Like a taste?'

I don't know what he will do if I refuse. I take a drop, realize that he might feel insulted if I reject his well-intentioned offer, and gulp down a little more.

'Hey, I didn't mean you to empty it.'

I start to explain that I wasn't drinking at all, that in fact I kept my mouth closed, but he is bright enough to check how far the bottle has sunk.

'It must be leaking,' I say, searching eagerly for a crack in the bottle. He snatches it from me.

'You look lonely. Wouldn't you like to come in with me and have a bit of fun?'

I start to explain that I am not lonely at all, and that if I am, then it's my own fault. He looks suspiciously at me, and I realize that he might have misunderstood me. I go on to explain in more detail, telling him that I am alone because I need to be alone. Fortunately, I manage to stop my eloquent discourse before mentioning my name. As long as he doesn't know who I am I shall find it easier to disappear without trace if he should try to drag me into something I don't want.

He has taken my refusal to mean that I have approved his suggestion. He puts his arm round my shoulder, probably without meaning anything by it: he is drunk and perhaps only wants to be kind to me. He drags me up towards the house, where the lights are on, and from which a most peculiar torrent of sounds is emanating.

Inside, it's even livelier than I had imagined. The sitting-room is not particularly big, but people are lying, sitting and standing everywhere. As I enter, I see a fair-haired chap get up from his seat, I hurry across and sit down on the corner he has vacated, hoping to be unnoticed there and able to take stock of the situation. The man who invited me has straight away disappeared again, perhaps he hadn't any right to bring me in, he might well have done it in a fit of thoughtlessness.

The fair-haired chap who had been sitting in my place before, returns and looks at me in surprise, while I stare fixedly in the opposite direction pretending to be the rightful occupant of this seat. Finally he moves away, shrugging his shoulders in such a funny way that I can't resist the urge to imitate him.

He joins a group in the middle of the floor, speaks in a loud voice and points a couple of times in my direction. There's a girl sitting opposite me, she smiles at me, perhaps she knows the man and is aware of what he's planning to do, perhaps she is simply amused by the way I moved my shoulders. She eyes me steadily, undisturbed and unembarrassed. I don't let that trouble me.

There's a girl lying on the floor with a young man on either side of her. The two men, who are as much alike as though they were twins, seem to be competing to see who can make the boldest moves without the girl stopping him. They go pretty far in their efforts to win, but the more crassly they behave, the more the girl simply laughs, louder and louder. I notice that the competition is not attracting anyone else's attention, and so I quickly look away.

The corner of the sofa which I am occupying, is just a little cramped. Two girls sitting by my side are kissing each other so fervently that they almost end on my lap. Because of the lack of space, my hand is at one time in danger of becoming involved in their caresses, but I manage to withdraw it, discreetly, and without disturbing them.

I have realized that a good deal of the noise is music issuing from a tape recorder. At some time or other I have had a glass thrust into my hand, I concentrate all my attention on it and on the music. Only after listening to it for some time do I recognize the song, some American thing about love.

The girl opposite, who differs from the others in the natural, relaxed manner in which she plays herself, is still looking at me. Perhaps she is merely absorbed in the music, for her lips move in time with the words. I think I can see them mouthing 'you and me'. She stares at me for a long time. I can think of nothing better to do than to look back at her. She smiles a little, and I, too, smile a little, although I am not entirely sure whether she is looking at me at all, or whether she is not rather dreaming to the sound of the music.

When the song is finished she gives me an angry look, perhaps I have been looking at her in a way suggestive of too much interest, perhaps she is offended that I have made no advances to her. She gets up and leaves the room. It looks as though the others are aware of what she is up to, they seem involuntarily to draw back, so she glides easily through the room.

The fair-haired lad who was originally sitting on the seat now occupied by me, has obviously explained to his friends what has been going on, and together with two or three others he approaches my corner. They don't even look directly at me, but simply drift closer. A girl in the middle of the floor begins to take off her clothes. The conspirators give themselves away by not as much as glancing at this performance.

However, when for a moment their attention is nevertheless distracted by the girl undoing her bra, I calmly get up and walk across towards the French door. They pretend that this doesn't at all thwart their plans.

The girl who was sitting opposite me is standing right in

front of the door. She sees me, smiles and makes to step aside. Something or other raises my hand and causes it to stroke her surprisingly soft hair.

STRI

There is no doubt that he is out for trouble, so I turn off and saunter further down towards the beach, quite calmly, without giving him the wrong impression that I'm afraid.

I can hear he's joined by someone else, and they are both following me. I have reached the water's edge where I pick up a couple of stones and throw them into the sea.

'He's picking up stones. He's throwing them into the sea one by one,' I hear one of them say behind me.

And then I hear two splashes soon afterwards. I whistle and saunter on.

'He's starting to whistle softly and he's walking on,' the voice says.

I turn round and cross my arms. I look benignly at them, in the hope of getting them to stop their childish tricks.

The slightly built youth I first saw stops, crosses his arms and looks benignly at me.

The other one, who is thick-set with curly hair, comments on my actions: 'He's crossing his arms and staring up in the air. He's rubbing his nose.'

I shake my head, slowly turn round and continue my way.

'He's shaking his head and moving on.'

I can hear the thin one just behind me, I can sense him imitating every move I make. The fat one is trotting along beside us, shouting out his comments.

'He's starting to whistle, but he's stopping again straight away. He's making a face because he's irritated. He's going on, he's increasing his speed a bit.'

I increase my speed rather a lot. I turn away from the sea, catch a glimpse of the slightly-built chap who is doggedly copying the way I walk.

'He's tapping his fingers against his thigh. He stops as soon as I mention it. He's beginning to swing his arms to and fro. He's jumping up on the greensward. Trying to ignore us. He's taking a couple of light, jaunty steps.'

He has seen aright. I have reached a hedge that prevents me going further inland. The only choice open to me is deciding which way to take along the shore.

The only sport at which I have ever been more than mediocre is the high jump. My last steps have had the effect of running up; I jump and, if not elegantly, at least in safety, I reach the other side of the hedge.

'I take a run and jump over the hedge,' I shout gleefully almost before I have landed.

The two are left behind. I hear one of them, the thin one, I think, attempting to force his way through the hedge, but in his state of intoxication he is obviously not capable of it, their voices fade away behind me.

'They're left behind with their tails between their legs, while I continue through the forest,' I shout back.

'I continue at a measured pace and skip with delight,' I comment.

'I notice I'm continuing to comment on my own actions. Now I'm turning left so as to get back to the cottage as quickly as possible.'

I smile a little on discovering that I have started to talk to myself.

'I listen, the voices are no longer to be heard. I swing my arms rhythmically, I change my gait as I comment on it.'

I shake my head at myself, try to make myself stop this nonsense, but all the time new sentences and new comments are popping up.

'I frown. Am I a little dissatisfied with the story I'm

creating at this moment?'

'I push some branches aside and emerge from the edge of the forest.'

I can see my cottage now, the small patches of light that show me the way.

Suddenly I stop. I sense a figure before me.

SALAM

'It doesn't sound particularly exciting,' exclaims Diam. 'So we'd better go in there. For we ought always to do the opposite of what would give us pleasure. Isn't that how you would put it?

'You're learning.'

While I am still trying to think of the sarcastic comment she deserves, she has taken hold of me and pulls me over to the car.

'You'll have to drive around a bit while I change. I'm going to wear what I've just bought.'

'Do you mean the nightdress?' I ask inventively. She doesn't even deign as much as to look at me.

Once more I have to keep my eyes on the road while her figure is revealed and slowly hidden again.

'You don't know what torments you are exposing me to,' I say sliding my hand over her bottom, which she has just wriggled out of the first layer of clothing. 'Oh, to want but not be able!'

She laughs and says in a didactic tone: 'In just the same way as it's more difficult to pass water when you don't have any to pass than it is to hold back for a moment when the urge is there?'

'Hey, I don't know you had literary pretensions.'

'Oh, but I do know my classics.'

As she is fastening the last button I stop outside the restaurant advertising 'cabaret every evening'.

Of course, the men have every conceivable reason to look admiringly at Diam, and of course the girls have every conceivable reason to look enviously at her as she enters the room, and of course I feel a certain pride at escorting her to the table to which the waiter shows us, but at the same time there's a touch of envy gnawing away at me, too.

There are already two couples sitting at our table. I'm about to put on some act to get a table to ourselves. But Diam stops me, and we take the places assigned to us.

The other couples at the table only just look up, nod and then continue the discussion on which they are engaged. One of them is rather fat, with bristly black hair. His cheeks are curiously soft and flabby, that is probably mainly what makes him look fat. He sets about staring unashamedly at Diam, only contributing a few inane remarks to a conversation that otherwise sounds quite fun.

He is obviously together with a girl with long fair hair. It is straight and cut in a fringe above her eyes. I notice that the others call her Agla. I try to establish a little contact with her, she looks at me with sorrowful eyes.

We give our orders.

'If Einstein had trodden on a drawing pin that morning, and if his tie hadn't got into a knot, he would have trumpeted some completely different conclusion. And then other scientists would have seized on it and found arguments to support it, proved it or demonstrated its truth. And the world would have had a different set of truths to live up to,' says the other man in the party.

While we are eating, the other couples go over Einstein's potential for changing, whether himself or the world. Before they reach any conclusion the lights go out, apart from those over a small platform. Here, a man dressed as a conjurer appears.

'He's got it up his sleeve,' is the witty remark of my bristly-haired friend. Agla quietly restrains him.

'It's not all that difficult to do what they call a conjuring trick,' begins the man in black. 'But it's against my principles to fool people, to pull the wool over their eyes, to bluff them, and isn't that precisely what all conjurers do? Ladies and gentlemen! It is my duty to conjure, and that I will do. But I wish to do it without fooling you.'

He hesitates for a moment, takes a card out and shows it to us.

'Just look. Here you see the seven of hearts. Now I will place this card out of sight in my sleeve. Have you seen it?'

He looks around benevolently, smiles to us good-humouredly, and again takes a card from the little table with his props.

'There, now we can begin. Here you see the seven of hearts.'

He holds out the other card. Then, slowly and meticulously, he tears it into little pieces and throws the bits into his hat, which he has first shown to be empty. Then, triumphantly, but to the amazement of no one, he takes out the card which everyone has known to be up his sleeve. He gratefully acknowledges the small amount of applause that is heard.

He continues with his strange performance in which nothing covert ever takes place, but everything is carried out directly in front of the public gaze.

At last he has finished, the lights are switched on again. The others at our table have now started discussing moral problems. Suddenly, the black-haired man leans over towards Diam and asks in a rasping voice: 'What about you? Are you good or bad?'

'Both,' replies Diam, laughing as she is taken aback.

'But you can't be both,' continues the bore. 'We've just agreed on that, you know.'

'*We* have not agreed on it,' I intervene. 'She is both: good to have, bad to do without.'

No one laughs particularly much at this, but Diam at least

glances gratefully at me.

As a welcome interruption, an old woman pushes her way across to our table. Her wrinkles are emphasized with black make-up, and she is dressed in a gaudy shawl.

'I tell fortunes,' she says, grasping Agla's hand. She looks intently at it and says something or other.

Then she takes Diam's hand and contemplates it.

'You'll receive a gift,' she asserts.

'Yes, it'll soon be my birthday.'

Diam laughs and draws her hand back.

The old woman has taken my hand before I can stop her.

'You'll have problems with the police,' she says and lets go in disgust.

She continues round the table. Afterwards she stands still with her hand outstretched, perhaps expecting us to tell her fortune in return.

The fat man puts a bottle top in the woman's hand and looks around in delight. As no one else is amused at his idea, he roars with laughter, as though by doing so he can justify his action.

He takes out a piece of paper. It is obvious that he is preparing some impressive revenge. As though he is on close terms with her, he leans over towards Diam and brays obsequiously: 'I couldn't have your telephone number, could I, Miss? I'm compiling a telephone directory.'

Diam feels some sympathy for the man and laughs benevolently at his joke. There is no roar of laughter from him. The rest of us look away. Diam continues on her errand of mercy. She fishes a ball pen out and writes down a number on the piece of paper he holds out to her.

As far as I can see, it is not the right number.

By now I have had a little to drink, so when Agla with the beautiful eyes turns to me and asks my opinion on the

63

question they were discussing before, it is not long before I start expounding the views I normally express. It is something to the effect that everyone can produce such a list of bad points from their past that they can easily come to see themselves as evil. But the opposite can also be done.

I feel that what I am saying seems quite logical, but suddenly Agla looks sharply, almost angrily, at me:

'That's rubbish.'

She starts saying all kinds of things that I have difficulty following. When she has finished, I give her a friendly nod.

'Yes, you might well be right,' I say reflectively, curious as to where my acceptance of such a new view will lead me. – 'I've not thought of it in that way before.'

'I'm sorry, I'm afraid I shall have to be going,' exclaims Diam suddenly, getting up.

'I'm sorry, I think we're going to have to go,' I say, getting up.

I scarcely have time to give Agla a friendly smile before Diam has disappeared.

I catch her up outside. She is alone. It is dark. Her dress shines out.

'That was a dull place,' she says.

SALAN

'It's not really enough,' I say.

'What do you mean?'

'We've only got a miserly three days together, so we can't waste a whole evening in some stupid restaurant, surrounded by uninspiring people.'

'No. What can you think of, then?'

'I've often dreamt of walking around in the streets, holding your hand and pretending that we belong together.'

'Well, then let's do that.'

There are not so terribly many streets, and there are not so terribly many people in them.

'I'll get tired if we have to go on like this for three days,' says Diam.

'I'd like to sit on a bench with you as well. Just sit and look at you.'

It is not too difficult to find a bench. We sit and look happily at each other.

'I'd like to talk to you, as well. Talk and talk for hours. But I can't think of anything to say. I have a feeling that it's simply got to be something pretty profound, and then it'll so quickly be boring. Or else it would have to be very funny, and that's almost even more boring.'

'We could just chat a little, you know. Just ordinary.'

'Yes: I miss you practically all the time you're not near me; I can hardly do without you.'

'I think you've said that on the odd occasion before.'

'Yes. When I miss you most of all I think: if only Diam were here, I could tell her how much I'm missing her.'

'Is that the only use you've got for her?'

'No, then I'll take her by the hand and walk up and down the streets, and pretend we belong together. And then I'll sit down on a bench together with her. And then I'll tell her ...'

'Thanks, I think I know how it goes on.'

'I could tell you how beautiful you are, as well. But that'll either be repetitive or rather forced.'

'Then it's best to refrain.'

'May I tell you a sad story?'

'Yes, if it's not too sad.'

'There was a man who was almost always happy; he was always busy with every conceivable task, and he was very interested in all kinds of things. Then, one day, he was given the famous message at the doctor's that he'd only got a year left to live. But the man was a well-balanced soul, philosophically inclined, so he took it amazingly calmly. He thought: I must make the most of the time I have left. Then he took a piece of paper to make a list of all the activities he was most reluctant to give up, those things he felt to be of the greatest importance to him. When he had sat for a whole day looking at an empty piece of paper, he hanged himself.'

'That was almost too sad.'

'Yes, I've kept some rather bad company. Perhaps I omitted to tell you that he was a friend of mine?'

'I wonder what made you happen to think of him in this situation?'

'That's hard to say.'

'Couldn't you make up for it by telling me a happy story, too?'

'Yes, of course. There was a man who was often sad. He was deeply in love with a young woman, but he couldn't win her. But one day he suddenly received the happy news that he would be allowed to spend three days together with the woman he loved.'

'And then the man took the girl over to a bench and said: Now I'm going to tell you a story about a man who was deeply in love with a young woman.'

'Yes, it could well end like that.'

'What do you mean by 'end'? I thought it had only just begun.'

'Joking apart: it is something of a burden to know that the next three days will contain the most important experience in my life. Every movement of my hand is something I shall remember, recall and re-experience to the end of my days.'

'I know what you mean. Can you see any way out?'

'No. Particularly now that we have talked so much about it.'

'I don't much believe in it, either. There's a train soon. Will you drive me to it?'

'Of course. Can you arrange things with Doria?'

'Yes, easily.'

There is hardly anyone in the streets, it's not far to drive, there are hardly any words left for us to exchange.

'Goodbye, Diam.'

'Goodbye, Alian.'

'If I give you a kiss now, it isn't because I want to think back on giving you a kiss now, but because I want to.'

'Thank you.'

The train is about to leave.

'There was one thing I wanted to try, but I didn't know that beforehand. That was to have you lying in my arm, to see you fall asleep, to watch your face while you slept, and see you waken up. I have experienced that. I'll think of that a lot.'

Perhaps the train has left before I have finished my sentence.

On the way home I drive more slowly than usual.

When I get home I don't straight away take out a sheet of

paper. On the contrary, I stuff all the sheets, both those on which I have written and the blank ones, into the hearth. I don't consider the fact that there are so many that some of them have to be left lying right out on the wooden floor. But I can't bring myself to strike the match.

SALME

Perhaps Diam feels the same. When she asks: 'What are you actually doing at the moment?', I am almost sure that it is her attempt to escape from this mood.

'I'm writing a little. And reading,' I say with a smile, because that is what I always answer. 'There's a couple of books here that I have been studying.'

I show her *The Man on the Road* and *What the World Showed*. She looks at them, without making any particular observation.

'I don't know them. Are they any good?'

'One of them is. Would you be interested if I told you about them?' I ask eagerly.

She is infected by my eagerness and sits down in anticipation.

'I only came across them by chance. But since then I have been busy studying the matter. Cloy Marel, who wrote *The Man on the Road,* lives somewhere in South America, I think he's in Chile at the moment, but he is constantly on the move, the various literature handbooks give a different nationality each time. He wrote three or four books before *The Man on the Road*. There's nothing special about them; they are a bit too fantastic, one of them is about ghosts or I don't know what. But then he suddenly went and got inspired and settled down to write this very beautiful and strange love story. It's about a girl who falls in love with a man she sees on a road. You ought to try it, I'm very taken with it.'

Diam is so lovely to look at as she leafs through the book that sometimes she almost brings me to a standstill in my explanation.

'The other one over there was written by G. F. Lanson. It's quite well known, although I don't think there's anything special about it. It's the first book he wrote. He's actually a farmer, living somewhere in the South of France. It seems he'd never thought of writing a book, but then, some years ago he was drawn into a curious affair, incidentally at the same time as Marel was writing *The Man on the Road*. When this interlude came to an end, Lanson felt that the course of events in it had been so amazing that he ought to write a book about it. And it turned into *What the World Showed*. It actually makes an authentic enough impression, and according to all accounts it recapitulates his personal experiences word for word.'

Now Diam has discovered it. She looks at me to be certain I'm not making fun of her.

'But it's the same book, of course.'

'Yes, that's what I discovered, too. They are identical, word for word. While Marel was sitting there inventing his story, Lanson was experiencing his. But even though their words are the same, the effect is quite different when you read them. Marel's is beautiful, flowing, and well thought out. Lanson's is a little dull and insignificant. Besides, it is pretty improbable in places.'

Diam has got up. I can see she is upset. She moves around silently and rearranges her things a little. She stops and looks at me, without smiling. I try to smile at her, but to no avail.

'I think I understand what you mean,' she says.

She is on the point of weeping. In order to hide this, she turns round and pulls out a sheet of paper sitting in my typewriter. She casts a quick glance at it, and then tears it in two.

'You shall have it as you wish. You would sooner be Marel, hidden far away from real life and inventing our love story,

70

than like Lanson being bound to reproduce the words we have already said to each other.'

She has taken her things. Before I have had time to think, she is standing by the door.

'I'm going now. I hope the story you invent will be a happy one.'

And indeed, she goes. The door closes. I see her hurry past the window, on her way up the road.

SALMI

'Why don't we do something?' I exclaim.

'What do you mean, Alian?'

'Why don't we do something about it, why don't we try to change it all. I want you, I want to live with you. A whole life, not simply three ridiculous days. And I want to stay with Mea, live a life together with her. Can't you feel that? All those possibilities that are being lost, incessantly. All those lives you are never allowed to experience.'

'Yes, I understand,' she says quietly. 'I sometimes have the same feeling, but it's no good getting worked up over it. You have to make sure of getting as much as you can out of the one possibility at your disposal.'

Something hurts deep down inside me. I don't mention it, so as not to give her any more problems. Instead I try to talk it out of my system.

'I want to live in peace and quiet with my books; I want to travel all the time; I want to meet new people; I want to be happy now; I want to be sad now. There are so many possibilities I *want* to try, but each of them demands a whole life.'

I don't know why Diam gives me such a worried look; I am merely explaining to her the situation such as it is. I don't want to upset her.

'Can't you hear them? Just listen. I can hear all the others. I can see them – where are they coming from? No, I won't sit down. I can't sit down when they come. Just look, see for yourself. They enjoy themselves, they suffer. There's one jumping over a hedge, there's one stealing a book, they're dressing up, they're coupling, they're quarrelling, they're

72

sitting on a bench, they're singing.

Why can't you see them, Diam? They're here. Where are they coming from? I can sense them.'

I can see that I am becoming calmer. I go on talking. I tell Diam about all those people she can't see. Perhaps she says she can't see them just to fool me, to make me forget them. I tell her about the girl who goes on staring at me all the time, about the girl with the big breasts and the twisted smile, about the girl with the sad eyes. They are here, and yet whenever I reach out for them they draw back from me.

As calmly as I can, I say that the others manage to try other possibilities, but all the while something is screaming inside me. I can't encompass them all.

They talk together, they burst out laughing, they weep. They sound hollow, they sound as though they have hidden in the vase. That's why I break the vase. I know perfectly well they're not in there. Diam hasn't understood that it was only to show her, to show what their voices sound like, how they try to get out.

Diam looks at me in a way that is not like her; in a dignified voice she says: 'I think my husband could be here at any moment. Will you wait?'

I shake my head until she has gone. But there she is again, different, saying sadly: 'Can you see a way out?'

She dances across to me, she laughs, she sits and eats with chopsticks and turns towards me, she drinks from a stream, she tears a piece of paper in two.

But it is not she. I have make a mistake. The wrong voices are coming from inside me. They must be removed before they do me any harm. I must cut them out.

Which Diam is it grasping my hand? I must get rid of them. I have to, can't she understand that? How can I explain it to her when she herself is one of them? I don't want to wreak destruction with the knife, I simply have to.

I can see that I'm cutting myself. I don't understand why I'm cutting myself. It is a good thing that Diam takes the knife out of my hand. Perhaps she'll help me to cut.

SANDA

I soon give up my ridiculous stance, bow deeply and respectfully to my friend the hall porter behind his glass screen, and go. I find a florist. I go in and ask whether I can buy a forget-me-not. I can't. Instead, I buy a large bunch of mixed flowers, and I get a beautiful white card into the bargain.

I select one of the flowers. The remainder of the bouquet I give to a pretty girl I meet; she has long, fair hair cut in a fringe just over her eyes. She is happy to accept the bouquet and walks on with it without turning round to look at me.

I take my single flower and tear off most of its petals, so that it looks pretty decrepit. On the card I write: My love for you will never fade.

When I get back to the hotel, I am received by a different hall porter.

'Will you send this flower up to Mrs. Levon, please.'

'Mrs. Levon no longer lives at this hotel. She has just left.'

'Did she leave a new address?'

'I don't think so, but I'll just check.'

He pretends to look through some papers, naturally without result. I have taken out a banknote and am holding it in my hand.

'But, wait a moment. It just strikes me that she rang to a travel agency just before leaving.'

I am given the address of the travel agency and forget my banknote as I hurry out of the door.

In the travel agency they remember Mrs. Levon quite clearly. She was to catch a plane to London; more than that they can't say.

I feel a little irritated during the long drive to the airport.

To my mind, she is grossly overplaying this part.

When I arrive they are kind enough at the Information Desk to point up in the air at the plane that is transporting Mrs. Levon to London.

By various circuitous routes, touching down and changing in various places, I reach London four hours later than Mrs. Levon's plane. But here the trail ends.

It seems pretty foolish to ferret about all over London in search of a girl whose address one doesn't know. I leave a message for her in the airport and go off to visit some friends.

I have now been thrown so much out of my usual rhythm that I stay for a few days. On the third day my friends introduce me to a couple of artists. During the course of conversation they mention an interesting girl who has recently arrived, a girl who paints some absolutely dazzling pictures.

That awakens my interest; they give me her address. The name on the door is Lowis, but it is Diam who opens up. She has her hair held in a band and is wearing a stained smock, but otherwise it's Diam.

'Hi, Diam,' I say cheerfully. 'I happened to be passing, so I thought I'd look you up for old times' sake.'

The girl laughs heartily.

'That's a new one,' she says. '"Haven't we met at some exhibition or other?" – that's one I've heard nineteen times. And then: "I think I know your sister" – that I've heard eleven times. But that one was so outrageous that you deserve to be allowed in for it.'

She shows no sign of recognition. That doesn't worry me much, so long as she receives me nicely. And that she really does. I don't get the chance to feel a stranger. We end up in bed, but the next morning I am thrown out.

I try to play up to the ridiculous role she has chosen, but it is no good. I try to make her stop her nonsense. Nothing helps: at eight o'clock in the morning I am out on the street, outside a closed door.

I visit her several times during the course of the day. Each time she says my idea was good enough for a single night, but I can't go on basing my life on it.

The following day and the third day I visit her again, with just as little success.

I try to discover who she goes around with, and then I go to great lengths to get myself accepted into that circle. It turns out to be quite incredibly closed. I can't combine two lines and make them look like a cross, so that none of these people is interested in talking to me about the art of painting. It makes no difference when I stoop to telling them that I'm an author. All I learn from them is that Lowis is only interested in one night stands.

I am by now so totally sick of the situation that I go to visit Diam to let her know that I'm going home. But this time her name plate has been removed, and her landlady tells me she has left, en route for Paris, she thinks.

By now I have spent so much time on this game that I would feel it foolish to give up. And so the following day I find myself in Paris without any trail to follow.

For some time I search around in artistic circles, and then in theatrical circles. But I hear of no one recently arrived corresponding to my description of Diam. I place advertisements in the newspapers, and even make enquiries from the police.

One day I am walking along a boulevard from where you can see the hookers touting for customers down in the narrow side streets. I come to a sudden stop on seeing an unusual girl in shiny red clothes leaning up against the door of a house.

I go across to her. Her hair has been cut, and she is wearing more makeup than usual, but otherwise it is Diam.

'Diam,' I exclaim in surprise. 'What are you doing here?'

'I'm called Jessap,' replies the girl. 'Can't you work out for yourself what I'm doing?'

It feels a bit wrong for me to have to agree a price with her before I am allowed to go with her. She lives in a small, expensively furnished flat where she seems to be perfectly at home.

She doesn't feel embarrassed towards me, but afterwards, when I talk of staying, she laughs at me. But I can come again the following day for the same price.

Humiliated, I come back the next day, and the next again. She appears to like my visits, but is still just as adamant in declining my suggestion that we should make the relationship permanent. She become angry, snarls at me when I start saying that she can't go on like this. She asks whether *I*, too, am out to 'save' her.

Her price is so high that I can't go on visiting her every day, apart from the fact that I don't have the strength to get value for money every day.

I am establishing a regular pattern for myself, although I have not reconciled myself to her profession and still think about getting her out of it, when one day, suddenly, she is no longer at the same place. This is not because she's got customers, but, as I ought to have foreseen, because she has left.

The next time I find her is in Rome. She is moving in those circles that still believe in the existence of the aristocracy. In some way or other, she has even managed to acquire the title of countess. Her dress and jewellery show that she has a great deal of money; as usual she dresses with a sense of style, elegantly, without too many frills. Only her hair is no longer allowed to come into its own; it has been taken up, and she usually embellishes it with jewels that seek to divert attention from it.

The countess turns out to be extremely unapproachable. It takes me several weeks before I am able to exchange a few words with her. But after a month has elapsed I am graciously invited to one of her famous soirées. I converse with her as inventively as is at all possible for me, and for the occasion I have put together a couple of stories that will flatter her.

Gradually, I gain more and more of her confidence. After a few more weeks I reach the stage of kissing her hand, which is quite a milepost to pass on my march forward.

Sweet is the moment when, finally, after the most exquisite attendance on her, I dare to kiss her lips. And even so, perhaps I have moved too quickly, for she refuses to allow me near her for the following week.

After the painful waiting of that week I receive a note, and finally I've made it.

Although the countess lags far behind Jessap in experience, and can't live up to Lowis' inventiveness, nevertheless I feel the night to which her note invites me, as crowning my searches.

SANDE

It's the hall porter who loses the battle. After staring vacantly in the air for a quarter of an hour he turns round and starts looking in some papers. He checks something or other in the register and settles down to reading his newspaper. He avoids looking directly at me. My tongue, meanwhile, feels quite dry and I have a feeling that it is swelling up. Now and then, however, he can't refrain from peeping out of the corners of his eyes to see whether I am still there. I am.

It is almost an hour before Diam comes down. She is about to say something to the hall porter, but notices me and comes out.

'You must forgive me,' she says, apparently upset. 'I put on all that act because I was hoping you would get angry and go. You see, you were such a long time coming back after parking the car. I met an old friend here in the foyer. And he invited me out this evening. I thought the easiest thing was to make you angry, so you would go; it was so you wouldn't feel hurt.'

'Me, hurt? You know perfectly well I'm not that sort. If you've met a friend and would rather go out with him, I see no reason why you shouldn't.'

I am just about to deliver my major lecture on the freedom of the individual and the most important thing between two people, but then I come to think of a comment I made in the car that upset her a bit, so I refrain.

'I'm glad you see it like that, too. I've got so much to talk to him about, and he's only here for the day; he's staying here at the hotel. When he's gone, you and I will still have lots of time together.'

She smiles and gives my hand a grateful squeeze that in a

way I am pleased about. She is wearing a dress with artificial flowers sewn on. Unfortunately, it doesn't suit her as well as many of her other dresses.

'Yes, well Hune – that's his name – he'll be coming for me in a moment. We're going out for a meal and a bit of a dance. What are you going to do? Isn't there a decent film on?'

'I think I've seen it. I'd better see about having something to eat, too. Incidentally, I assume it wouldn't bother you if I went with you to the same restaurant? I mean, in view of the way we look at things.'

'No, you'll be welcome, if you like. But I'm not sure you'll be keen on the place Hune was thinking of.'

'I don't care where it is, as long as I can get something to eat. It's nice we can both take it in such a relaxed manner. A situation like this would doubtless give a lot of people a whole host of problems.'

Hune drives up in his big car. He greets me brimming over with enthusiasm, he is on the point of saying that I am just the kind he best likes to pinch a girl from. But he doesn't say it.

He gets Diam on the front seat together with him, while I spread out on the back seat. Diam and Hune don't seem to be so relaxed with each other as I could wish, but the drive is too short for me to be able to settle down and sleep in a natural way.

He is quite good looking, almost too good looking, with a gentle appearance and a gentle voice. While he is parking the car and I am alone with Diam I am on the point of asking her whether she is really sure he's a man, but I realize that such a remark could easily be seen as an expression of jealousy.

In the restaurant I immediately select a table well away from theirs. It is made of solid wood, but it wobbles every time I draw my breath. I eat my meal and pretend I only have a passing acquaintance with the charming couple sitting at the other end of the room.

Diam sends me a friendly smile a couple of times. And the nice chap that is me waves merrily back to show that he is enjoying himself, and that whatever she does, she mustn't let herself be disturbed by his presence.

Nor does she. It's not long before she is out on the dance floor with Hune. He hugs her pretty violently, probably so much that it seems a little out of place in this exquisite restaurant. But they have so little time; he is only here for this one day.

A man comes along and sits at my table. He offers me a drink.

I refuse politely. – 'At one time it would have been different,' I explain. 'I've drunk a fair amount in my day. But I've stopped now. I discovered that it was slowly wrecking me. First I lost interest in one thing, you understand, and then in another. But for heaven's sake don't let me put you off, that wasn't the intention. By all means go on drinking, it's no concern of mine how you are.'

Without another word, the man orders two glasses. Soon afterwards, his girl friend, a powerful blonde, turns up and sits down beside him.

Hune's prowess on the dance floor has resulted in one of Diam's artificial flowers being torn from her dress. Discreetly, I pick it up and pass by the couple on my way out to the toilet.

I hear Hune explaining that there are country people who are not doing very well. Diam nods, grateful for this information. I don't want to disturb an important conversation, and so I deliver the flower so tactfully that only Diam discovers it. She is kind enough to thank me with a warm smile.

When I return, she is giving him her telephone number. – 'You can always give me a ring, and we'll work something out,' she is saying in a friendly voice.

I don't want any more to eat after all, and so I go out and take a taxi.

SANGE

She is lying just in front of me when I waken up the
following morning. I think of what it would be like if that
were the sight meeting my eyes when I opened them every
day. Would it be able to ensure that every one of my days was
beautiful and festive?

I remember a fairy tale about how the day will reflect the
first thing you see. It tells of the man who in the morning
wants to run out to the most beautiful spot in his garden so as
to open his eyes there, and so has pulled his nightcap right
down over his eyes to avoid seeing anything less beautiful
beforehand. I can't remember whether he's lost his nightcap
during the night, or what the point was. Perhaps there's an old
witch waiting for him in the garden?

There is every prospect of *my* day being delightful. Whereas
during our first day I made a great effort to be inventive in the
belief that I had to entertain Diam, I decide to let this day be
relaxed and ordinary.

We spend our morning walking hand in hand through the
streets in the town. A couple of times I become so enraptured
about her that I have to stop and convince myself that it really
is she, and that she is standing before me.

An elderly gentleman is offended by the obvious delight we
take in each other. He says reprovingly: 'Remember you are
in a public place!'

Laughing, we hurry back to the hotel.

In the afternoon I ring Mea from a telephone box. With an
admiring eye on Diam, I tell her that I am in town to buy
some carbon paper and so just want to make use of the
opportunity to ring her. I grumble that it's impossible to get

even carbon paper in Dahle: this trip is taking the best part of an afternoon for me.

In the evening we go to the theatre to see a comedy by Sheridan: *The Critic*. We maintain a respectable distance from each other because in this place there is a big risk of meeting people we know.

I have become accustomed to people staring at Diam, but here it seems to me that people are not only looking, but are amused, which I find remarkable. Until I discover that in the rush – it was almost too late before we left the hotel – I have put on my jacket inside out.

I hurry out into the toilet and turn it.

The value of the performance is greatly enhanced by the fact that I am sitting in such a way that I can follow it at the same time as I can see Diam in profile. I can follow her eyes, her expressions, and secretly hold my hand against her body. I can almost say that I experience the performance as though we were one.

When the play is over we go to a restaurant nearby. We choose a simple, solid meal. While the first day's dinner was light, exciting, as new as our meeting, today we need more ordinary food.

We talk for a long time, at first a little about the performance, which we both liked, and then about ourselves. I feel that after only two intimate days together we already know each other in a quite different way from before.

In a flash I realize that in the course of today we have entered into something like an everyday relationship, whereas during the first day we had been playful, sensitive and new to each other. For a moment the thought shocks me. But when I realize how lovely this ordinary day together with Diam has been, my mood is completely transformed. It is no wonder that we could have a good time together when we faced each other open and with open minds. It is all the more impressive that, as we progressed towards everyday life together, we could still mean so much to each other.

This thought let me go on savouring the joy it was to sit together with Diam, to go with her to the hotel, to see her undress, to go to bed with her, even though these actions no longer were new to us, but a repetition of what we had done the day before.

SANGU

I t is like the continuation of the most beautiful dream when the following morning I open my eyes and see her face before me.

I kiss her eyelids, she smiles in her sleep, wakes and puts a hand on my cheek.

She gets up, moves in slow motion, her hair billowing out behind her. One item of clothing after another floats down around her slender body, is drawn in to it and encompasses her greedily and gently.

Later, when we are in the lift, I have the feeling that it's moving upwards, but when we stop we are nevertheless at some version of the street.

The houses glide smoothly past us, and people move to make room for us. I don't know where it's coming from, but there is a gentle music in the air that makes Diam's steps still lighter, still more dancing.

We reach the forest and allow ourselves to be drawn into it. We stop, Diam leans up against a tree. I trace the lines of her face with my finger. For a long time it continues to drink in the impression of her, continues until it has got to know her down to the slightest detail, continues until it can remember every feature in dreams.

People pass by and see our happiness, they smile at us and move closer together.

We go further into the forest, where we are entirely alone. Diam speaks, her voice is soft, as though she were whispering in my ear. She talks about us, too, and says that she has been looking forward to today, right up to today. She says it feels as though we have been allowed to borrow an extra life, a life that was lying around anyhow, but to no avail. That we were allowed to borrow it because we had an excess of happiness with which to fill it.

Then we reach a little stream with slowly running water. She bends down and lets the water fill one hand. She raises it to my mouth and lets me drink from it. I kiss the hand when I have emptied it, and again bring a smile to her lips.

In the ground just above the water's surface I trace with a finger: You are Diam, you are lovely.

I borrow a kiss from her lips and imprint it above the name. With two branches and two stones I build a little dam, so that the water rises. It reaches my message and drinks it in. I remove the dam so that the water can flow on and spread my message throughout the world.

We go back through the forest. All the houses have been painted to receive us, the sky has been polished and the air dusted.

The hotel comes to meet us, and carries us up to our room. We fall asleep without for one moment having let go of each other.

And yet it is even more beautiful the next morning.

'What shall we do?' says Diam.

'I'll lie on the wide white bed while you walk around the room. Your nightdress billows out behind you and only finds its rightful place when you stop. Your legs are long and bare.'

'What shall we do now?' asks Diam.

'You come over to me. You sit down on the edge of the bed. You bend down over me. You seal my mouth so I can hardly speak. You are warm and smooth.

Now you lie on the bed while I walk around. You lie stretched out, with your legs slightly bent, with your arms above your head. You turn a little before I manage to say more, and pretend you are asleep.

88

I stop at the wash basin. Taste the water that already bears the taste of my message from yesterday. I go back to the bed and sit down beside you.

You begin to speak. You are suddenly impassioned and sit up. Your hair hangs uneasily because you haven't brushed it. You go and brush it while continuing to talk. You stand with your back to the cupboard and speak. You fall silent and smile. Toss your head. Now your hair falls softly.

You begin to dress, speaking the while. You ask me what clothes you should put on, although you've nothing to choose from.

You ask whether we shall spend the whole day in this room. I say that it's a good idea, suddenly you become filled with ardour. I say that you are beautiful when you are impassioned. You come across to me.'

Evening falls, and the character of the room suddenly changes. We dress. We leave, holding each other by the hand, apprehensive like two school children on their first day at school. We pay the hotel bill.

We are silent most of the time as we walk through the streets. Every now and then we embark on a rather strained conversation that we both know is just an excuse.

Diam's train is already at the platform. I embrace her, hold her tight, determined never to let go. And let go straight away.

We smile a lot. We do not say that it has been lovely. Countless thoughts rush through my mind, but none suggests a way out.

Diam gets into the train, she stays in the door. I close my eyes, I don't know what I wish.

STOLE

Now I want to discuss a piece of apparatus I once saw in a museum.

It was a kind of game played with ball bearings, in a big box with glass sides so you were free to see inside. At the top a ball bearing drops into the game. It lands right on a nail, bounces up again a little, perhaps falls back on to the same nail, and repeats the process, but sooner or later it has to make up its mind: it has to allow itself to drop either left or right of the nail. Here, it soon comes up against a new nail that it lands on top of. Once more, the ball bearing must make a choice - will it go to the left or right of the nail? It continues its course, constantly coming up against new nails and thereby new choices, and it ends at last at the bottom of the game where there is a long row of compartments. If, for instance, the ball bearing has chosen to jump to the left of each nail, it ends in the compartment furthest to the left. If it has chosen to jump to the left every time except the last one, when it jumped to the right, it ends in the second box from the left.

If you let a single ball bearing fall through the system, then, it has complete freedom to choose which compartment it is going to end in. As an interested spectator you have no chance of knowing where it will go. On one occasion it might choose to come to rest in the middle, on the next two to come to rest far out on the right.

But now, in this museum, they allowed not one, but countless ball bearings to fall. As far as I remember, it was a question of thousands of ball bearings. Every single ball bearing among the many has its freedom, decides completely independently in which compartment it will end. But strangely enough, it turns out that, even among ball bearings, there are norms determining how to position oneself. For despite the freedom of each individual ball bearing, they work together to such an extent that every time the experiment is carried out they nicely arrange themselves together in such a way that they form the same pattern. (And this is something rather resembling the hat Napoleon wore: a lot in the middle, and fewer and fewer out towards the sides).

I think I stood for more than an hour in front of this contraption. I watched excitedly as the experiment was repeated time after time, as the thousands of ball bearings were allowed to follow their own course until they reached the bottom. Every time I hoped they would choose to arrange themselves in a new pattern, that once, every single ball bearing would have decided to make for the middle box, or that some right-wing fashion should arise among them so that all the compartments on the left would be under-supplied. But every single time I was disappointed.

The longer I stood in front of this ball bearing game, the more hypnotized I felt as a result of the movements of the residents. So fascinated was I that it was as though the ball bearings were being transformed before my eyes, transformed into tiny round people who, with precise, metallic clicks landed on points of equilibrium and then without hesitation bounced up to one side and passively let themselves fall further down to the next critical point.

I was totally absorbed by my fantasies, and when I suddenly felt someone nudge me, I felt as though I myself were inside the apparatus. I felt the breathtaking fall until a transverse peg stopped me and felt the staggering sequence of thoughts that flashed through my mind during that short time before I had to reach a decision and allow myself to fall to one side. Every time I struck a peg I was aware of temptations pulling me on one side and others pulling on the other. I had to fight the most furious battles before overcoming the temptations on one side.

I again received a nudge, and became aware that I was in fact standing on the wrong side of the glass plate, that I was only watching the game. The nudge stemmed from a distinguished-looking elderly gentleman standing by my side. He was half bald and wore spectacles. He pointed with his walking stick at the game, which he had obviously been watching for a long time.

'All of which goes to show that for ball bearings as well as for human beings there are fixed structures from which they are not able to deviate,' he said.

'Yes, but all of which does not exclude the possibility that each ball bearing has enormous difficulty in discovering the path that has been determined for it, that it must suffer and twist and turn to find its way down into a compartment. By watching a lot of ball bearings you discover something about ball bearings. But a person who knows something about ball bearings knows nothing about *one* ball bearing.'

He considered my reply for a time. He really appeared to be interested in understanding me.

'I don't quite follow,' he said. 'Isn't it more valuable to know something about ball bearings than about a single ball bearing? That might be skewed or scratched or totally unpredictable!'

'I believe,' I said and was sorry to attach such importance to my words, for I could also well understand his personal attitude. 'I believe that it is not so important that people are not free, provided mankind is free.'

His face lit up in a smile.

'Ah, now I understand you. You mean it doesn't matter if

we are all condemned to leap into an abyss, provided we each individually choose to do so?'

STOLI

I can now understand that it implies a lot more.

I put myself in a situation where I have to choose: Do I want coffee or tea? And hey presto, I am two persons, I am one drinking coffee and one taking tea.

That opens the flood gates, for all possibilities, all the possibilities I have dreamt of. At last I can come to live fully and wholly, live all the lives I have had to renounce.

If the world has become so all-embracing, so rich, why should I then sit here in an out-of-the-way cottage and waste my time. There is nothing to prevent me from getting up and grasping all the possibilities.

But that is what I am like, I know myself. I sit a little longer, 'to think things over'. Here, where no mistakes are possible. For I can choose exactly what I want. And I can go on choosing, no choice will be binding, because I will always be experiencing the other possibility as well.

There is only one mistake possible: To stay here, to go on speculating, to put off, to fail to grasp the world and try life.

There are no limits any longer.

I can rape a girl. If, later, I am caught, I will simply say that it was not me, but another of my segregations who did it. I can safely go out and steal: if I am caught, what does it matter when I can simply go on living in all my other ramifications?

This thought makes me dizzy. It is so unexpected, so vast, so revolutionary. Only now, with me, with my discovery, does mankind really exist, exist in true freedom.

There are a few individual things that don't fit, but that is because I can't yet see the uttermost consequences of it all. Not because my understanding is letting me down; it's rather that

I feel that my body can't keep up with my mind.

I wrote 'my' discovery, for I feel very strongly that this Olvin Quer whom I mentioned before, to whom the honour for the discovery will quite rightly be ascribed – I feel in a way I can't define, but about which there is a curious certainty, that he is an earlier segregation of myself. Why should he not be? He certainly resembles me, in his life and in his urge to rebel against it.

And another thought strikes me. They come so quickly that I have difficulty in controlling them and sorting them out. Who knows if the other writer, too, Carl Sinistre, was not one of my segregations; perhaps by now he is only a distant ramification, but that doesn't rob me of the honour. Incidentally, honour means nothing, only the results are of any significance. How could I in the shape of Olvin Quer work so closely together with someone else, Carl Sinistre, if we were not both segregations of the same person? This is the proof. Our unique cooperation was so effective because we ultimately came from the same place, from the same hopes, the same despair.

I'm amazed that I am the only one to have seen it. I must try to formulate it straight away. No, the excitement gripping me will not let me. I must exploit my discovery now, instead. I won't waste my time any longer with these empty, lifeless sheets of paper.

It is obvious to me now what must be my first action in the new circumstances; the choice is not difficult.

I'll fetch Diam. I'll drive over to her. She must have gone south by now, but I'll find her all right. I can reach her in nine or ten hours. I can be together with her by midday tomorrow.

I'll fetch her, I'll fetch one of her segregations, the most beautiful, or the most engaging I can find, if there is any difference. There must be. She must be there, one of them

95

must be there. The wisest, or the kindest. She can be allowed to decide for herself. Her husband can keep a different segregation, or two, if he wants. No, if Diam wants.

No time to be lost.

STORE

I would like to add a few comments on the thoughts I had before I began writing this book.

At that time I'd had two books published. One in which, with a beginner's self-assuredness and vulnerability, I had hidden myself and my opinions behind layer upon layer of ironical veils. And a second, a work in which scarcely a word or thought was my own, in which everything was taken from the literary predecessors whom I most admired. In the first book, with the help of ironical frills I had argued in favour of perpetual uncertainty. This was aided by my use of irony, which I employed in order to explain (subtly) that certainty was an evil, and the fact that I knew nothing was not the only thing I knew. In this book, I moreover took pleasure in letting myself end up disagreeing with myself.

The second book, disagreeing with the first, nevertheless had one feature in common with it, and that was the fact that I didn't make assertions or express views here, either, that with any confidence could be ascribed to me: someone or other was always placed between me and an opinion. On the contrary, I tried to present myself as the sum of the models I might think of using.

I felt now that in my third book I must try to express myself, to discover myself, my own words, my own opinions. This turned out to be no mean task. If I had an idea, it was either so banal or so hazardous that I would only dare to express it to the accompaniment of a scornful expression of derision, or else it was obvious to me that I had not myself conceived the idea, but had taken it from someone else, a philosopher, an author or some quite different source.

This was what I constantly met with: irrespective of what door I knocked on in the hope of finding myself, I discovered an empty phrase or a quotation. It seemed obvious now that I would have to write a novel about my vain search for my identity, but even this obvious possibility seemed so tainted that I couldn't conceive of it as my own, and so it had to be rejected.

But when I had weeded out these empty phrases and quotations, there remained one single feature which I could view as my own, as something characteristic of me: this urge to write in my own way, to discover what was my own, my personal view, despite the fact that I totally accept that I am nothing in myself, that I am only a hole filled in with bits and pieces of Kafka, Sartre and my neighbour (wherever he got it from). Or, in short: my urge to turn myself into something that I am not. (As Sartre has already so wisely put it, at least more or less).

This book is about me and my attempt to understand myself as the sum of my potentials.

The dilemma reveals itself in the linguistic field, too. As you see, my original aim of writing 'as myself' results in a chaotic mixture of genres. This is a consequence of the fact that all my potentials, all the I's into which I could turn myself, each demanded its own language and its own tone in order to express its 'self'.

I would like to try to illustrate this, to view it in a different way.

The other day I attended a play which convinced me of the bleakness of all things. In all its painful nakedness, I saw the emptiness of my life, my vain occupations, my humdrum daily round. And not only did my own dreariness appear clearly to me, but I also became aware of the dispiriting behaviour of my acquaintances, the difficult, wretched lives of my friends, and of their desperate and vain attempts to flee from them on festive occasions. The truth of this play forced its way to the bottom of my soul.

However, only a few days were to elapse before I came across a book which in turn captivated me – a charming description of love, a tender dance on delicate new grass. My eyes were filled with poetry, the night air became balmy, the world became a light, effortless drama in which I was one of the actors. This book showed me a picture of the world, a picture that was true because I could make my own world resemble it.

I scarcely need add that, rather less than a week after this event, I was taken by a quite different mood. By turns, my world becomes hopeless and then radiant, incomprehensible and chaotic, and then exciting or grotesque, sometimes simple, sometimes trivial. Naturally the books I read are only one of the things that set my view of the world in motion; the events into which I am drawn can just as easily change the colour in the projector illuminating my world.

In my present mood I feel like writing a book attempting to recreate the hopeless world introduced to me by the drama which I have just mentioned. This view of the world would naturally make me choose my words in a quite specific way. But I would scarcely find the task really satisfying. On the one hand, of course, I would be more or less copying the drama to which I refer, and on the other I would only manage to present one of my many possibilities.

Similarly, I would like to reproduce the world as the love story made me see it. To do so, of course, I would have to choose quite different words, an entirely different style. But the idea would suffer from the same faults: it would be derivative, and it would be too narrow.

In order to avoid both defects I would have to write a book

like this one. It's a kaleidoscopic picture of the possibilities I have felt within myself. It's original in the sense that it presents the very worlds in which I have moved, and it's comprehensive in the sense that it doesn't limit itself to portraying just one or a small number of the moods with which I am most familiar, but it presents my world as a series of flickering moods.

STORM

B ut why has the book acquired this form?
The structure is unusual, although it is not unique. Certain similarities will be found in Michel Butor's novel *The Labyrinth of Time*. Although it is a single-stranded story moving from beginning to end, there is a gradual build-up in it that is perhaps reminiscent of the segregations in this one. In *The Labyrinth of Time* it is the experiences of the principal character at different times that are combined, and the ramifications are based mainly on time, whereas it can be said with some justification that *Life at Night* is based on spatial separation. A further feature that these two books have in common is that they are narrated in the first person and that they are concerned with the narrator's attempts to understand himself.

Outwardly, Svend Åge Madsen's short story 'The Poor Narrator' makes use of exactly the same form as this novel. In the short story we are concerned with a man standing on a square who segregates into two persons, one of whom leaves the square, while the other remains behind. Both persons again segregate several times. But although, outwardly, there is some resemblance, the fact that the short story by its very nature is forced to limit itself to quite brief episodes results in a significant difference between it and the novel. The short story is told in the third person.

In a short story entitled *The Crossroads*, Cloy Marel tells of a man who segregates into soul and body. The principal object of the story is to illustrate the philosophical theory that a person's body and corpus are two distinct mechanisms that chance to correspond to each other in just the same way as two alarm clocks can show the same time, though without being connected with each other. In *The Crossroads*, one of the alarm clocks gets grit into the works, and so they make divergent choices on reaching a crossroads. The soul continues, in the first person, to the left, while the body, in the third person, turns right.

On several occasions Jorge Luis Borges mentions the idea of writing a book that ramifies, without having done it himself. In *The Garden of Diverging Paths* he talks of a book that divides up ad infinitum, thus presenting every possibility conceivable. And in an analysis of Herbert Quain's work he describes a book entitled *April March* that I haven't been able to find anywhere, in which the chapters ramify backwards in time. Finally, in his story *The Theologians*, there are two characters who are, as it were, segregations of each other, mirror images of each other.

In its simplest form this idea has often been seen in literature, most commonly in the sense that the reader is presented with a plot that finally splits into two or more possible conclusions.

So other stories in the style of poly-analfables are known. (A poly-analfable is a story with more than one ending/exit). So what use is made of the form in this particular instance?

You can't simply be content with the view that the book is a perfectly ordinary collection of short stories, containing 32 stories which happen to have some of their beginnings in common. As a curiosity mention can be made of the fact that, before *Life at Night*, the author had written a book that was so voluminous that he couldn't find any publisher willing to take it on. The form used here saves a great deal of space. If we put each section at 3 pages, we have 32 stories each consisting of 6 sections, that is to say of 18 pages, which under normal circumstances would take up 576 pages. These 576 pages have here been encompassed within 63 sections $(1+2+4+8+16+32)$

of 3 pages each, that is to say 189 pages.

The form will probably be more easily understood by a consideration of this author's previous books. He has published two.

The first, called *Beginning*, is about a man existing at one and the same time in a youthful and an older version. The young one lives partly a realistic life and partly a dream life in which he imagines himself as older. In the same way, the older man lives his own natural life, and in addition a life based on memories (distorted, one imagines) of his youth. These four life stories are woven into each other, contradict, travesty and parody each other.

Alian Sandme's other novel is called *Together*. It is about a world in which there are three different sexes. For a love affair to be consummated there must in this place be three representatives, one of each sex. In a rather complicated pattern of events, the book describes the intrigues and conflicts arising from an instance of adultery, a crime passionnel and a masquerade. Everything is told as seen through three eyes (the inhabitants of this place are one-eyed).

The present book has in common with the two earlier ones the fact that it contains several different stories, several different threads of action which, according to normal logic, can't all be correct. From this it can be deduced that, with his use of unusual forms, the author is trying to say that the world is not unambiguous, but self-contradictory and paradoxical.

As for content, the three books betoken a certain progression.

The first concentrates on the individual. It is the narrator and his relationship to himself that is the dominant theme in *Beginning*.

In *Together* the 'characters' never achieve any independent status, they are only viewed in their relationship to each other, never exist for their own sakes. It is society or the world as a whole that is the theme in *Together*.

In his everyday life the individual human being must necessarily experience himself as an individual, as a special being who cannot be subsumed with others. It is impossible to see yourself as a secondary factor in society, as a factor in history, as a factor in a particular process.

Philosophy can apply this point of view and consider totalities and vast structures, but thereby it will necessarily lose sight of the individual, however determined it may be also to encompass the living human being.

Good literature enables us to experience this strange duality, which is a precondition for our really being able to understand mankind: we can follow an individual, see him as a factor in a vast pattern, a machine that is made up of other living beings. But we also experience this individual's 'own' life, we experience his sorrows and joys.

After *Beginning* that was about mankind, and *Together* that was about the World, I must consider this book as an attempt to achieve a fusion of the two themes. It could be said that it is about the most essential thing, about Man in the World.

After these reflections I think we are in a position to propose an interpretation of the book.

STREG

S he turns round, as though she had expected me to do this.
I feel irresistibly attracted to her; perhaps there has been
something or other in the glass, but at the same time I have
gone so far that I daren't draw back, for fear that she might
feel slighted.

Uncertainly, I stroke her hair again. I draw her head
towards mine and realize that I am kissing her. She returns my
kiss.

Suddenly, I become aware that I have completely forgotten
myself. In order to extricate myself naturally, I explain that I
need to go for a walk. To make it sound more convincing, I
ask whether she would like to come along too.

I don't allow myself to be surprised when she says yes. My
arm happens to be around her shoulders, I leave it there, and
so does she.

We go down to the water's edge. I don't know what can
have happened, I feel terribly remiss, though it doesn't really
bother me. It is as though I have stepped outside myself, found
someone else to be, someone else who is more suited to this
girl.

Her shoulders are frail. She walks on looking straight
ahead. I ask her if I might ask her name. She says she is called
Kerianne.

I don't quite know what to say to her, because I have a
feeling that I have so much to tell her. Instead, we stand still
and kiss. I find it very difficult to stop again, but I force myself
so as not to weary her.

We walk on in the loose sand. It's not all that far to my
cottage. I tell her about it. Tell her enough for her to be able

to find it. I am not interested in forcing her to come along, perhaps she is afraid of what I might do if she declines, so I don't suggest going there. But if she should want to, she must be able to find it from my description, another time, I would prefer her to make up her own mind, if she wants to come.

She seems thoughtful. Perhaps she is wondering how her friends are. She smiles at me so that I shan't think she has regretted coming with me. I suggest turning back. She doesn't protest, and I understand that I have guessed right.

We walk in the loose sand, where we only make slow progress. Twice I happen to stop and kiss her. Her body is slender.

She looks lovely, she speaks nicely to me and gives me a very friendly smile. But nevertheless I don't feel that that is what makes me stop and look at her all the time. I would like to tell her something about this, about what else it is in her that makes me behave in this way, so that she can better understand me, but I can't find any suitable words.

'You are ever so Kerianne,' I say instead.

We are close to the house where I met her. I am not keen on going back. If she wants to laugh together with her friends, I would prefer not to be there.

'I must go back to the cottage,' I tell her. 'I've got some work to do.'

'At this time?' she says with a smile.

My first impulse is to tell her that I am writing a book, and that I am very busy. But I'm afraid she might think that I am saying it in an attempt to show off, and besides it wouldn't be true. I remember that I have my ball pen, quite an expensive one, in my pocket. I take it out without her noticing it, and pretend it has fallen out of my pocket. I pick it up.

'Oh, that's what it was. Would you like it?'

She nods and appears to be pleased with it.

'I'd love it. That was nice of you.'

'It'll soon be used up, in any case.'

'Well, even so.'

We kiss again, and say goodbye. I stand for a while and watch her walk back to the house.

STREN

'Keep your fingers to yourself?' she says, making to smack my hand, which is already gone.

'Take it easy. There was a bit of fluff.'

I hold out a piece of fluff and flick it away before she sees there was nothing there.

'Sorry if I seem forward,' I say. 'But have you had that dress for long?'

She looks at me uncomprehending.

'I'll explain. I'm a dress designer. This very day, I've designed the dress to end all dresses. So much of it is routine work, you know, but today I wanted to make something absolutely original and personal, something for the very special woman. You'll understand that I was surprised when I saw you dressed in the model I designed this afternoon.'

'That can't be true, I've had it for a long time, for a couple of weeks, at least.'

'No, of course that's not the one I designed. Someone else has been quicker than I. May I?'

I flutter my hands with what I think must be professional movements, I appraise the cut of the neck and the sleeves.

'That's incredible,' I conclude. 'Oh, yes, just one little detail.'

I crouch down and appraise the waist.

'There's no difference at all,' I say. 'That's a day's work wasted.'

She is becoming suspicious. I hurry to add: 'That was why I was sitting looking at you like that, I'm afraid I've been indiscreet, I was really only thinking of the dress. Oh, I'd better be going, otherwise I'm afraid the tomato will burst.'

'The what will burst?'

'Oh, that's a long story. Shall we sit down?'

We sit down just inside the door. Meanwhile I have the opportunity to work out what my expression might mean.

'The tomato is my friend,' I say. 'We live together in the same flat. He's both very red and plump. As the result of a mistake, well, it's a sad story really, but he was operated on and had his regula appetitus removed. It's an organ of some kind, something to do with hormones, it's what makes us stop eating when we're full. We'd invited quite a few people round this evening, 8 in fact, to a women's admiration meeting.'

At this moment I glance shyly aside and am about to come to a halt, so that she has the chance to take note of my expression.

'But we had to cancel it, after all the food had arrived. And now the tomato's left at home, alone with all those goodies, and without this regulator to tell him when to stop.'

'What kind of a meeting did you say it was?'

'Did I say something about a meeting? Oh, its just an expression we use. I'm sure it's of no interest to you.'

'Yes it is, won't you tell me about it?'

'It's not quite decent, to be honest. I don't like talking about that sort of thing to a girl I don't even know; you'd only get quite the wrong impression of me.'

'I'm called Parliette. Now we know each other a bit.'

'I'm called Sjera Zade,' I say quickly. 'I'll tell you about it on two conditions: that you don't let it go any further, and that you don't get the wrong idea of me from what you hear.'

'I won't let it go any further, but it won't be easy to know whether the thoughts I'm having are wrong ones.'

'You can confidently assume they are. Oh well, but I'll probably never see you again, so I'll tell you for the sake of your bright eyes.'

Some of the guests are going, so by now we are sitting more or less undisturbed in the sitting room. I don't make the slightest effort to touch her.

'We're a few guys who get together now and then for what we call a "women's admiration meeting". It could just as well be called something else, but you can't very well say that aloud. At such a meeting every participant has to tell a story or describe an experience or conjure up the portrait of a girl, we can do as we want. Afterwards we have a vote on which of the contributions has given us ... well, you must forgive me, which contribution has managed to produce the biggest ... in short: we select the story that has been best suited to producing an erection. Well, of course, it's done in all innocence. Sometimes we have a girl there as a sort of prize for the winner. But, as I said, it was cancelled today, so now I've no use for the story I'd prepared.'

The beautiful Parliette is no longer completely indifferent, although she is still far from making approaches. She asks about the story I've been planning. We've started to drink, at least she is showing no sign of wanting to go. I spin out my daring yarn pretty well to make it convincing enough, and I manage to weave it into a completely different kind of story. It's a sad tale about a beautiful young girl. At no stage do I suggest it is about her, but I borrow from her as many of my heroine's attributes as I can manage. I can almost see it is having an effect, and Parliette is beginning to be touched by herself.

Of course, almost too naturally, this account merges into a story about a man suffering need, a man unable to find the girl who can teach him to love. I have a feeling that she is on the point of understanding what I am up to, so for a change I weave into it an anecdote about a man who sells his motorcycle for one match in exchange for the first spoke, two for the next, four for the third, and so on.

Parliette's cheeks are burning; we are the only ones left in the room, most of the guests have left, the rest have discreetly withdrawn to an adjoining room. Now I reel off a story that I have actually made up before; it's more piquant than risqué, but nevertheless so piquant that the listener's sinful thoughts will scarcely be able to lie dormant.

When I have been telling stories for two hours I am glad there don't seem to be another thousand nights. We have made ourselves comfortable, lying side by side on the sofa, in all decency of course, even though Parliette's hands do appear to be a little restless when my stories reach their climaxes. I give an envious thought to my near namesake, whose only duty was to tell enthralling tales. That is only half of my task: I must at the same time contrive to tell my stories in such a way that she is softened more and more, and so that her interest in me is awakened more and more.

I seem to have everything under control. When, in the course of a touching little detail I have the misfortune to lay my hand on her side, she twists and turns cautiously so my hand slips further on towards her breast.

When I come to the story about the man walking about naked in the snow outside his house because his mistress has locked him out, we feel so cold that we involuntarily move closer together.

And finally, when I read the description of the woman whose skin was so soft that hands simply *had* to touch it, then, at last, my hand slips under her dress.

STRID

I realize that my eyes must have deceived me. And yet I am a little uneasy as I approach the cottage.

Soon I am no longer in doubt. Through the thin curtain I can see the figure of a man. He is sitting, apparently reading, in the chair which I vacated a short time ago. I wonder whether it might be one of my friends who has decided to pay me a visit – several of them have the same habit as I of sitting up far into the night. One of them might have wanted to surprise me.

I am quite near the house now. I can't see any other cars apart from my own, and the man doesn't look like any of my friends. And yet he seems familiar to me. He is sitting quietly reading his book, the same one I was reading before I went out.

I have got right up to the cottage. I find a gap in the curtain. Something is wrong. Suddenly, I know where I have seen this man before. I have met his face in the mirror every morning.

For a moment I stand in complete confusion, looking at myself in there in the chair. That was the person I least of all expected to find in the cottage, no wonder I had difficulty in recognizing him.

I stand undecided. The man inside puts down the book on his lap, takes the paper I have left lying there and makes some notes. He hesitates, adds something. Then looks up and smiles in satisfaction.

I remain there undecided. He takes the book again, settles himself more comfortably. He seems to feel at home in the cottage.

At last I am able to pull myself together. I go round to the door and convince myself it is locked. While searching for my key, I wonder how this man, whoever he is, has got in.

I clearly remember locking the door and putting my key in my pocket before going out, but it is no longer there. Feverishly, I go through my other pockets, though I am in no doubt as to where the key should be. Unsystematically, I kneel down and examine the ground near the door, obviously without result.

Suddenly, I remember the inexplicable jolt I felt when I reached the shore. Though without any particular reason, it seems obvious to me that I must have dropped my key when I bumped into this other person.

I go back to the window and knock on it to attract the man's attention. He reads on, unperturbed. I knock louder, shout, but without result.

I try another window closer to him. Finally, he looks up, but only to go across to the fireplace, poke around in it, and settle back in the chair. I dance around outside, shout and bang on the window, in the hope that he might look in my direction before sitting down.

In desperation I take a stone and throw it at the window. It hits its target and falls to the ground with scarcely a sound, and without damaging the glass. I take a bigger stone and fling it violently against the glass. According to any natural estimate the stone should, without the least bit of difficulty, have smashed the window, but as was the case with the first, if drops quietly to the ground after striking the glass with negligible effect.

Nor is the sound loud enough to attract the man's attention. Once more, I try both doors. I take my jersey off, wrap it around my hand and aim a powerful blow at the window.

I feel a slight pain in my hand, but the glass holds. I run around the house a few times, I shout and I kick at the wall. For a long time the man goes on unconcernedly reading his book.

I try to get into the car, but that, too, is locked. I intended using the horn or driving it in towards the house, I don't know what. I try to tease the car door open, but to no avail.

I reach a desperate decision: to clamber up on the roof and force my way in through the chimney. I immediately give up my plan on account of the height of the house, and because I am afraid of being suffocated by the smoke.

Suddenly, I have an idea and run down to the beach. I search in the darkness for the spot where I felt the unexpected jolt. I think I more or less find the spot, but I don't find the key. Nor am I in any doubt that the man has taken the key and gained access to the cottage with it.

I have a feeling that my blows on the window have become even weaker; at first I could produce a noise like branches striking the glass, but now it's only like a shadow raising its hand to it.

The man carefully examines the notes I made last. He leafs through the closely written sheets of paper on the table. He strokes his beard and ponders. He leafs back and forth through the pages again. He sits down and now writes a long, continuous passage, breaking off occasionally to stare up in the air. Finally putting down his ball pen, he gets up. He remembers something, goes back and takes the pen and a blank sheet of paper, and puts both in his pocket.

He looks at the fireplace, apparently convincing himself there is no danger of its flaring up. He puts out some of the lights, but, as I usually do, leaves some of them on.

I place myself ready by the door. He comes straight out and would have bumped into me if I had not jumped aside. He locks the door, apparently without seeing me. I say good evening, but he does not react. I shout, he looks up, but only to see what the weather is like.

I position myself in front of him so that he can't avoid seeing me. Nevertheless, he starts walking, straight towards me. At the last moment I jump aside.

He makes for the beach.

STRIM

N ow I must add some information on the male figure that appeared to me further along the road.

It is someone I have met in the district on several occasions. My first meeting with him took place a number of years ago. At that time I was pretty pleased with myself and thought I was pretty good-looking; I had nurtured my intellectual gifts and could be quite witty. I was just about as satisfied with myself as a young person ought to be. For although I am convinced of the duty constantly to try to improve yourself, I also think it important always to ensure you have put yourself into a condition of which you believe you need not be ashamed.

Thus I was in harmony with myself when I attended a party where I met this Iego Askaron whom I found both charming and pleasant to be with. He was very much like me in an immense number of ways; he was well read and quick at repartee, although he didn't make exaggerated use of this. He was well groomed and well liked. There was only one point on which he differed from me. He had a certain manner of intonation that made him more convincing and, I admit, a little more charming than I was.

I am not the type to be envious for such a trivial reason. On the contrary, I valued the experience that Askaron had given me, and I made an effort to speak with the same intonation. To my own credit I must say that I succeeded rather well.

The next time I came across this man was a chance meeting in the street, where he was chatting to two ladies whom I also knew. I stopped, exchanged a few remarks and then carried on.

But this meeting was not without its effect on me. In the course of the brief conversation I had noticed a feature that Askaron had acquired since our first meeting. It was nothing very much, merely a special way of moving his hand, a gesticulatory movement which I found rather sophisticated. Hardly did I get back home before I was standing in front of the mirror and practising this movement, making it a part of my natural way of expressing myself. The great similarity between him and me made it easy to add this little detail.

I think I felt pretty near to perfection now, that is to say I believed I had developed my potential as far as could be hoped. But the very next time I came across Askaron I came to a different conclusion. This time he had recently read a book about which he told me elegantly and amusingly, and which added yet another dimension to his charm.

Naturally, it was not long before I had read that same book.

Now you might be inclined to think that I would feel a certain bitterness towards this man who time after time inflicted a minor defeat on me, but this was not at all the case. I welcomed such guidance as he could give me. Moreover, it must be remembered that our meetings were not so frequent, and that the superior virtues he always displayed over me were so slight that they were quite easy to emulate.

For he continued to have advantages over me. I soon developed a clear insight into the special quality that could not help but differentiate us from each other. It might be a way of laughing, a confidential way of addressing people, a way of standing and observing a group of people, a way of nodding in understanding, or it might be a new way of sitting down, a new colour to add to one's dress, or a way of looking deep into the eyes of the woman you were talking to.

I could constantly learn new tricks from him. Taken

separately, they might seem insignificant, but gradually, and thanks to the many new qualities and characteristics which he conveyed to me, I became a different person, just as he, too, naturally had changed.

Sometimes I didn't see him for long periods, and then I discovered that the characteristics which in the meantime I had added to my personality, were characteristics which he, too, had found it appropriate to acquire, though naturally there was still one respect in which he was still ahead of me.

Thus, I have chased around after this man for years, and every time I have met him I have been curious to see what new feature he could provide me with now.

Perhaps inspired by my meeting with the man on the pole, perhaps as a result of my realizing how messed up my life is, this time I feel particularly interested in what Askaron has to teach me.

I follow him in the hope of catching up with him and managing to have a conversation with him. On the way I remember a dream I had recently, in which he played a part. I have only a vague recollection of the dream, but I do remember that it ends with my suddenly finding Askaron dead one day. The shock of this experience is so great that I immediately feel weak and sense that my strength is leaving me.

SALAMA

'We'll find something a bit less dull,' I promise optimistically.

We climb into the car and drift back and forth along the few streets. The only place that looks as though it would like a visit from us is the department store, which is open.

We park the car some way away from the no-parking sign. We stroll around in the shop, pretending to be slightly intoxicated. At the same time we buy all the most ridiculous little things we can find, a thingumijig to fit bottle tops on again, a magnet for holding a comb on a mirror, and various unidentified objects. Diam's bag gradually becomes so heavy that I am given the prestigious task of lugging it around.

We end in the book department. From habit I look around to see whether they have one of my books. Diam laughs at me. I am a little hurt that they don't have a single one of them.

For the past few minutes we have been followed by a chap of sinister aspect. At first I thought it was Diam who was the attraction, but his persistence makes me convinced me that he is the store detective. Now, he is engrossed in a volume of strip cartoons.

I select a rather splendid book, bound in red leather, which looks as though it is one of the most expensive in the store. I walk to and fro for a while, holding the book almost hidden by Diam's bag.

It is quite amazing how uninterested the detective can look when he makes the effort. When I am afraid that he won't be able to stand the excitement any longer, I go over to the counter. He clearly becomes confused. I take the book out; the detective can see that I am talking to the assistant about the book; the detective slouches off in disappointment.

'Ah,' I say to the assistant, pretending to take the book up from Diam's bag. 'I have a book here I would like to change.'

The assistant looks suspiciously, first at me, then at the book. I painstakingly shut the bag again, but it is probably mainly Diam's innocent appearance that convinces him.

'What would you like to change it for?'

'Well, have you Alian Sandme's latest book? *Together*, I think it's called.'

'No, I'm afraid we don't have it.'

'That's a pity.'

'No, it's supposed to be rather over-long,' he says smartly. 'But, mind you, I haven't read it.'

'Could you order it for me?'

'Yes, certainly. What name am I to order it in?'

'That's up to you. But I'm called Elan Tric Sibera.'

It ends with our leaving with a credit note for the expensive book, an order for my own book in a name I have forgotten almost before we are out of the shop, and an assistant looking suspiciously at the gap in the shelf in which the magnificent book fits perfectly.

When we reach the car there is a ticket fixed to the windscreen wiper.

'The prophecy,' says Diam and is amused.

I take the ticket, which indeed is a greeting from the police, and dutifully fix it on the next car in the row, which has not been given a ticket.

We have gone a good deal of the way to the cottage before Diam discovers that she has left her ball pen behind in the restaurant we vacated in such a hurry. I make an energetic protest when she wants to go back for it. As though it were an argument, she points out that she got it from me long ago.

From this I seek to prove that it must be almost finished; she only looks at me.

The restaurant seems about to close when we arrive. I run over to the door to get in, and at that very moment it opens and I run my head into something or other.

The blow is so violent that I sit down, or rather I look up into Agla's worried eyes when I make to get up. My head is throbbing.

Diam and a few others help the chap with bristly hair to get up. Luckily, his head has obviously suffered just as badly from the blow, for he's holding it in his hands.

In some way he looks different from before. He gives Diam a look as though he already owned her. He is on the point of making some crazy remark about having hit the nail on the head, the nail being me. He irritates me dreadfully. He tries to appear intelligent. He speaks in a distinguished voice.

'He's got it up his sleeve,' I croak.

None of the others can see anything funny in that. I roar with laughter on seeing the ridiculous faces they put on.

He leans on Diam, pretends he is weak, and at the same time makes eyes at Agla.

I put my arm round Agla and draw her close to me. But then there is Diam, and I stop.

I don't know whether I'm drunk, or whether it's the blow. I feel somewhat unaccustomed to myself. If I had any hope that he wouldn't run off with Agla in the meantime I wouldn't mind making a bid for Diam.

But Agla looks at me with her green eyes.

He gives me a bloody condescending look, as though he's planning to run off with both girls. I remember something about a ball pen and take a step forward. He has obviously also had an idea, for it happens again: our heads smack into each other like two billiard balls.

It is Diam who helps me up. In return, it is Agla who supports him. My head is one huge lump, and it is spinning.

I don't know how long I have been out, if I have been out. I hardly know how many times we have banged our heads together. It feels like three or four, but something convinces me that a smaller number is more likely to be correct.

He smiles foolishly, and croaks some idiotic remark. He follows it up with one of his characteristic roars of laughter.

'There's no ignoring him,' I say quietly to Diam.

She smiles and places a hand on the tender spot, it is so lovely that I don't tell her that it makes it hurt more.

Agla gives me the occasional look, but then she is suddenly busy again helping the fat man, who is moaning and making a general fuss.

In my hazy condition I become aware of some dilemma within me. A desire at the same time to drive home with Diam and to put an arm round Agla and go off with her. Still more hazily I sense that this possibility would only double the dilemma.

I imagine myself on my way to the car with Diam, and see the bristly-haired chap clutching heavily at Agla. The thought is terribly disturbing to me. I picture myself putting my arm round Agla, looking into her eyes, and then see the fat man leaning in over Diam and starting to grope her. I begin to feel sick at the thought, or perhaps it's the accident.

Luckily no one asks my opinion. With a supportive arm and a firm hand, Diam leads me across to the car and puts me inside.

'Now you stay there and be quiet, and don't get yourself into any further scrapes, while I fetch the ball pen.'

As tame as a groggy boxer I nod and follow her with my eyes. I see her stop near the group around the fat chap, pass an odd remark to him, place a hand in blessing on his bristly hair, and go into the restaurant.

She is right. I sit there quietly.

SALAMO

I place my hand on her shoulder.

'Let's go home,' I say. 'That at least won't be dull.'

I say this in a warm, convincing voice. Had the moon been shining and making my teeth gleam, it would have been perfect.

I take the rug from the back of the car and place it over her legs, although it is a great sacrifice to have to do without the sight of them.

'Are you comfortable?' I say gaily.

She nods, and we drive off.

We have not gone a third of the way when Diam discovers she has forgotten her ball pen in the restaurant.

'We'll ring to them and ask them to keep it,' I say comfortingly, as she really seems to be worried about this little thing.

'They won't bother looking for a ball pen if you only ring about it. Would you mind taking me back to get it?'

'Of course not, if it means so much to you.'

Diam stays out in the car while I go inside to fetch the ball pen. In the foyer I meet Agla coming out of the toilet. She looks as though she's been crying. She turns towards me, and I have a feeling that she needs to talk to me.

I hesitate, and smile as encouragingly as I can. Then I continue into the main room, comforting myself meanwhile with the thought that I probably couldn't have helped her in any case.

The fat chap is sitting there, drawing on the tablecloth with Diam's ball pen. As far as I can see in my hurry, he's produced a whole row of naked girls.

'Excuse me, but I think my wife has forgotten her ball pen,' I say, looking around.

'Yes, it's here,' says Agla's companion, handing it to me.

I thank him, apologize for disturbing him, and leave. Agla is nowhere to be seen.

Diam is waiting in the car, and gives me a grateful kiss when I hand her the pen.

This time we get home without further mishap.

We arrange ourselves now with a view to staying in the cottage for the time left to us. Diam suggests rearranging some of the furniture, and that immediately heightens the cosy atmosphere in the cottage which until then had only been intended to provide me with somewhere to sit and write, and a place where I could sit and read.

It amazes me how big a difference her presence can make. I get her to sit down and take out Cloy Marel's book *The Man on the Road*.

'As a little token of how happy I am that you were able to come, I would like to give you this book. I'm very taken with it, and I think you'll like it, too.'

She is surprised, but accepts it without making difficulties for me.

'That's nice of you. I'll read it before long.'

'You know I love books,' I say earnestly. 'The ones I like least are those you can quickly run through. They're like a journey by train, they take you quickly and reliably from one place to another. That's what they can be used for, they're useful, but often a bit boring. From a distance there's not much to distinguish them from each other. I have a far higher opinion of books that are constructed so that you have to wander around in them, books that present you with a universe which you have to explore for yourself. I enjoy making my way into that sort of book, trying to find a thread going through it, coming up against an unsuspected hurdle, being led astray by some tempting passage, being forced into regions through which I have already passed, but which now appear to me in a completely different light. These books are like a walk in an exotic, unknown city, useless, but usually exciting or challenging. You never get to know them entirely, and when you have left them you only need to close your eyes in order to recall the moods through which they have taken you. *The Man on the Road* has been such a book for me, and so I'd like to give it to you. When *you*, too, have read it, it will have even more value for me, for then we shall have travelled through the same region and can recall the same experiences.'

I am in no doubt that she will appreciate the book, and that she will look forward to sharing its experiences with me.

But she has to leave it aside for the first two days. During that time we arrange a life together, every minute taking part in the other's life. And with every hour we spend together, I learn something new about her, meet an unexpected and beguiling aspect of her character, discover constituents that I have not even suspected before, find regions of great beauty which I have never before uncovered.

And although it seems difficult to have to part from her, we now both have a sense of having lived together through a story, right to the end. It seems to me that by our common efforts we have guided our relationship through a complicated labyrinth, and that we have reached this temporary conclusion by choosing the very road that seemed the right one to us.

And when we part, we are determined to close our eyes often, so that, although divided in space, we can re-live these days.

SALAND

D ear Diam,
I had a strange experience on arriving home at the
cottage. After taking you to the train. After seeing it disappear
with you. After driving home alone.

I had sat thinking for a long time. I wondered why we had
not been able to manage it, why we couldn't simply be
together for three days, what I had done wrong.

I don't know how long I sat with these thoughts. But it was
a very long time. I didn't do anything to control them, just let
them buzz around in my head, let them go round in circles, let
them run around exactly as they wanted.

I re-experienced the short time we were together, minute by
minute, scrutinizing every moment to discover when I went
wrong. And suddenly, it was as though I could see a complete
pattern, a network with a lot of junctions, all of which contain
the possibility of making a wrong choice. How can one choose
the right way in this pattern when one has never learned the
rules, when one doesn't know according to which principles
the choice must be made?

It reminded me of a game of hunting the treasure we
sometimes played as children. One of us, or just as often a
grown-up, had worked out a pattern. At the start of the game
all we other children were given a piece of paper, the same
piece of paper. Two possibilities were written on this paper. It
might say: Look in the middle sandpit on the old tennis court
or on top of the grocer's slot machine.

And off we went. Some of the children placed their faith in
the sandpit, others in the slot machine. In the sandpit, the first
group finds a new slip of paper indicating two new hiding

places. Again they split up, some choosing one, others the other. The same thing happens for the children who have run to the slot machine. They, too, must choose individually between two possibilities, choose in the dark, or as optimistic children say: try their luck.

And so the game goes on, through all kinds of ramifications, each of which scatters the children yet again. Until the pattern is finally finished with a single one of the clues showing the way to the treasure, which was a little prize for the lucky child, while all the others, sometimes as many as thirty-one or sixty-three, come to a dead end.

As you might imagine, I wasn't particularly good at this game, and I don't remember ever being the lucky one. When, on one occasion, I myself arranged the treasure hunt I ruined it by letting the clues go round in circles, which entailed the risk of having to search to all eternity. Incidentally, it wasn't really a disaster, for on top of everything else I had made the end of each line a dead end. So there were no winners in *my* game.

Sitting alone, with all my thoughts buzzing around in my head, I felt that once more I had been the loser in a treasure hunt, but this time it had been a much more fateful game, for this time it was my life I had played wrongly.

Diam.

When I had got this far in my considerations, I remembered one of the characteristics I had as a child and which I had almost forgotten; I probably deliberately suppressed it because I didn't like it.

I wrote before that I was never the lucky one in a treasure hunt. But even so, I was often the one to find the prize. As you will understand, it could easily happen that there were not sufficient children for one to come to the end of each line. So we all risked finding ourselves in a blind alley, while the treasure had still not been found. I now developed a knack of quickly forming an overview of the junctions that hadn't been used. I leapt, as it were, across the entire pattern and landed in a completely different set of possibilities. Of course this was cheating, but I had to do it; if I wasn't lucky as a matter of course, I had to be cunning instead.

Diam. I intend putting this letter in the place where we once used to leave our messages for each other, in all probability you will come across it by chance.

I merely want to suggest to you that I might be allowed to cheat in our game, that I might be allowed to leap over into another junction, and be allowed to try again. The fact that I didn't find the right way the first time doesn't mean that I will never be able to find it. On the contrary, it means that I have a better chance of finding it next time, for now, at least, I know one trail that leads nowhere, and *that* I can avoid. I find my fraudulent behaviour all the more forgivable as I am the only participant in this game – as far as I know – for which reason my leap in the net of fate does not deprive anyone else of the honour.

This letter has been difficult to write.

You are in no doubt about my feelings for you. I couldn't gain anything by putting them into words.

I had no excuses for my actions, I can't put my finger on any one place where things started to go wrong. I can't see why I ought to have done anything differently.

My sole explanation is the one I have tried to give you here: that I am living in the dark, and therefore must accept that sometimes I can take the wrong turning.

Alian.

SALANE

S uddenly, I am able to tear myself out of this mood. I throw down the box of matches and start laughing at my emotional behaviour. I received a bunch of flowers I hadn't expected; now I'm tearing my heart out because they withered rather quickly.

Once more I take the road back into town. My condition is grotesque, on the surface I am light-hearted, singing and at the same time beating out the rhythm with the foot on the accelerator pedal, so that the car proceeds in sudden spurts, but beneath it all there is a sad, dark resonance that refuses to go away.

I make straight for the restaurant that Diam and I had thought too dull. Only when standing in the foyer do I hesitate, wondering what I really intend doing in this place.

While I am standing there on the point of regretting my hasty decision, a girl issues from the toilet. She seems upset, and looks away so as not to let me see she has been weeping. At that moment the door opens and a man enters. The girl looks at him, waves happily to him and makes to go towards him, but the man only vouchsafes her a quick glance and goes on into the lounge.

The girl is left behind, even more miserable than before. I go across to her and without further ado ask whether I can help her. She shakes her head, but does not retreat.

'Will you give me the pleasure of going a short walk with me?' I say, taking her hand. 'I'm rather upset; perhaps you wouldn't mind listening to me. I don't think I can find any better consolation than having you hear what I have to say.'

She draws her hand away and then replaces it in mine.

'I can't,' she says. 'I would like to. But there's a man in there. He'll be furious if I don't join him.'

'We'll go just a short way,' I say and take her along with me.

We walk along the paths in the garden. She seems to be at ease and on edge at the same time.

'Are you frightened of him?'

She is on the point of weeping, but checks herself.

'He's malicious and foolish. I can't stand him. He's just been taunting me while all the others were listening. He humiliated me, made me look ridiculous.'

'But why do you put up with it?'

'I've got to. No, don't ask any more, it's no use. No one can help me. It's impossible.'

We have sat down on the edge of the fountain. A gentle breeze blows a little spray over to us. I kiss away two drops that have settled on her eyelid.

'I'm in his power. I can't get away from him. I am subject to an evil fate.'

The situation is so unexpected to me, both so distant and yet so real. I realize that the path that seemed so fortuitous and haphazard, meaningless and confusing, has irrevocably led me to this place.

'Perhaps it would help you to tell me about it.'

'There's no escape, but it does me good to know you show interest. I feel better now, let's go in.'

'Won't you tell me about your difficulties first?'

She settles herself more comfortably, and gently supports herself on my shoulder. She smiles gratefully to me.

'I can't imagine any better occupation than hearing a long story from such beautiful lips.'

Before she starts to speak, we kiss each other gently, and the fountain scatters its blessings over our heads.

SALMER

When I keep in mind the fact that my concept of the world is not the world, can I then be reproached for choosing to live in the more pleasant of these two possibilities? With what right can I be indicted if I prefer to live in my imagination?

As I get up from the table I find myself wishing that Diam could see this, perhaps then she would better be able to understand me. She must soon be up at Dahle, from where she can take a taxi.

But why am I interested in the Diam who is following an uneven path, when I have just realized that I can perfectly well prefer the Diam I can fix here on paper?

Something feels wrong.

I take down Marel's and Lanson's books. Look at them as though the responsibility is theirs. I put them into the fire, but before the flames have reached them I pull Marel's out. With a certain satisfaction I see the flames take hold on *What the World Showed* and see it go up in flames.

Having chosen as my world the one in my mind, I can, by committing to paper what my thoughts are centred on, give a picture of my world.

I can't help thinking of the event in which one of my colleagues was implicated some time ago.

He is a good friend of mine, and has been writing for many years, but he has only published a small number of things which, nevertheless, have been of very high quality.

He lived very quietly, visiting Mea and me a few times together with his wife, but normally he kept to himself, and worked very energetically at his writing, slaving away harder than most authors I have known, rewriting, improving, rejecting.

Suddenly, my friend completely changed his behaviour. He became quick tempered, irritable, and later melancholic. He seemed not to be working any longer, but would wander around town for hours on end, sometimes just up and down the same street.

I was told that his wife had fallen ill, and saw this as the reason for his changed manner. I tried to establish contact with him in the hope that I could be of help to him, but he rejected me categorically both on my first and second approaches.

After some time, his wife died. His behaviour was still just as unnatural. He didn't seem to have started drinking; for a time he could be quite silent and withdrawn as he used to be, only to break out then in the most furious self reproaches, after which he again resorted to his hour-long walks.

Some time after the death of his wife, when I thought he must have composed himself again, even though he had been profoundly affected by his loss, I managed to arrange a meeting with him. There were just the two of us present, and I began to appeal to one of his better selfs.

It was quite obvious he was not listening. I had a feeling that one of his attacks was coming on, when he suddenly leaned forward in his chair and looked at me with flaming eyes.

'I'll have to say this to someone,' he exclaimed hoarsely. 'You'll be able to understand me and my problem. You must listen to me. You must promise me not to be curious about any points I mention here; you mustn't try to acquire further information, not against my wishes, and you mustn't try to change what I want or to pester me to go further than I wish.'

'No, of course, obviously not,' I said, eager to learn what he might be about to tell me.

'A vague promise like that isn't enough. You must promise it, solemnly and in all sincerity.'

I had to repeat my promise, as solemnly and earnestly as I could, before he was satisfied.

'You know that I used to work hard at writing and made great efforts to improve my writing. As I imagine you yourself do.

A couple of years ago I had an idea that caught me right from the beginning. As you know, once you have made a start, you can write a whole lot of books by simply repeating the first one. This method had never appealed to me. When I had managed to express a view in one way, I consistently tried to find a completely different approach to the same problem. In this way I was always confronted with new difficulties, for which reason I wrote a great deal, but published little.

Now I had the idea that if a writer prepared sufficiently, planned precisely and carefully thought through every single detail, if he worked sufficiently conscientiously and meticulously, it would be possible for him to arrive at the perfect story.'

He buried his head in his hands; I was afraid he wasn't going to be able to go on with his account. His manner of narrating, which I cannot reconstruct so as to do justice to it, had possessed me in some curious way; I felt he was enmeshing me in a net of words.

'Of course, I was prepared for the task taking years, even the rest of my life,' he went on. 'That didn't worry me. From the moment I had the idea, writing the perfect story became my sole interest.

- I undertook a thorough study of the classics. I carried out countless stylistic exercises; I researched, I planned. And suddenly, one day, I wrote. Far sooner than I had imagined, I reached my objective. You can't imagine the condition I was in when late one night I put the last full stop to my story. It was beautiful, it was a perfect work of art, it contained everything, and yet it was simple, but first and foremost it took possession of one; you often use the term captivating of a story – that term could be used with total justification of my story. You know that as an author you don't quite feel the power of your own work, but even so, I was in no doubt that with this story I had achieved my objective.

I was completely worn out, and fell into bed. The next morning, as usual, Eza read what I had written in the course of the night. She became obsessed by the story. She woke me up, something she did not usually do, and praised me for it. For the remainder of the day she was rather silent and thoughtful. The very next day after she had read it, she asked to be allowed to see it again, and she was even more captivated by its beauty and profundity. And so it went on. The following day she had to see the story again. On this occasion it made her depressed and dejected.

I still didn't suspect that anything was wrong. I was simply delighted at the interest she was showing in my work, and I carefully noted the emotional changes to which she was subjected. One day the story would fill her with delight, so that she was laughing exuberantly most of the time. The next day she was captivated by its poetry and increased her own charm thanks to its power. But the story's power over her didn't diminish with the passage of time, as I had expected, and soon she had to read it several times each day, soon she knew large sections by heart and repeated them to herself during the intervals when she was not reading. She became incapable of sleeping, couldn't spare the time for it, and likewise she stopped eating.

Soon she began to waste away, there was no way in which I could get her thoughts away from the story. If I took it from her by force, the wasting process simply seemed to accelerate. At last she died, with the final words of the story on her lips.'

My friend was no longer looking at me. He delivered his explanation looking up in the air, as if he had done it countless times before.

'Nor is that all. Naturally, I was horrified, and hid the story when I saw what effect it had on Eza. I carefully ensured that neither doctors nor visitors caught a glimpse of it. But I couldn't be a hundred per cent sure. An inquisitive nurse had gathered so much information from Eza's confused words that she became interested, and one night she gained access to the drawer in which it was locked up.

The poor nurse obviously read it through, perhaps a couple of times. We shall probably never get to know. The following morning, she was found with shining, feverish eyes. All that they could get out of her was that now she could see the whole world transfigured and radiant, that she understood everything. She had to be confined to an asylum and has been there ever since, and no change has been seen in her condition.'

My friend had no more to say. He suddenly refused to say any more. He gave no explanation as to whether his disturbed condition was due to self reproaches on account of the damage his story had caused, or whether, especially, he was tormented by having the perfect story lying in his drawer, and not daring to have it published.

He got up and left before I had been told whether the story was even any longer in existence. He left, and since then I have not managed to talk to him again. His behaviour is more or less as it was before, although there are signs of a little progress.

Quite often I find myself envying Eza and this nurse, who have had the unique experience of reading the story. The thought has struck me that if it can be written once, then it must also be possible to write it again.

SALMET

I wait until Diam is out of sight. Then I go out and start the car and drive gently after her.

When I catch her up, I open the door and shout: 'Are you interested in a lift into town?'

She climbs in.

'No, I'm not going to town, I'm going to the airport.'

'That's not much out of my way. I'll take you with pleasure.'

We have only driven a short way when Diam says: 'You are so fond of stories. Would you like me to tell one, which I guarantee I haven't experienced myself?'

'That doesn't sound very exciting, for what haven't you experienced? But I'd love to.'

'It's about a man. So are most stories, as you will have noticed. There aren't many stories about women. They're only used as supernumeraries and background figures in stories about men. If you make up a story about a man's sufferings and complexes and efforts and successes in his efforts to get into bed with some woman or other, then you call that story *A Woman's Song*, and pretend that it is she who is the principal character, while she really only acts as the keyhole through which the man finally had to go.'

'I actually agree with you,' I say. 'But I rather feel that the fault lies with the women. Stories about men are what can be expected of men. The fault lies with the women who never get around to telling stories about women's difficulties and successes in their hunt for a man. But I thought you were going to tell me a story about a man.'

'Yes, but you side-tracked me. This man always played

roles, like so many of us nowadays; that's what you have to do now.'

'I'd sooner say that one can't help doing so,' I interrupt pedantically, as though I have just read a book.

'Yes, I know. But, you see, that extraordinarily nice man I'm talking about was quite aware that he was playing roles. At the same time he entertained a reckless urge always to be honest.'

'You really do know some unusual men.'

'This man simply had to demonstrate his honesty by all the time revealing the role he was playing, for otherwise, of course, he would be deceiving whoever he was together with. This man didn't say to a girl: "I love you." He said: "I am treating you now in the way usually referred to as loving." At a party, when he was telling quite a reasonable story, I once heard this man suddenly interrupt himself in order to say: "Now I'm probably playing the part of the know-all."'

At the moment I need to play the role of someone who feels that the cap fits.

'The man I'm talking about could well say to his girl: "I love myself in my role as your lover."'

Again, I try to introduce a remark to the effect that I have understood her, but she continues mercilessly.

'The man I'm talking about could even think of saying to his girl: "I'm not particularly good in a role as a happy lover, because that means that I have all the time to adapt my role to you; I much prefer myself in the role of your unhappy lover, for then I can invoke the most touching aspects of my emotional life."'

'Diam, I love you.'

I manage to surprise her. I don't think I'd ever said it to her. She turns towards me in a surprised silence.

'Now what's the title of that role?' she asks when she has

collected herself.

'When you ask directly, it's called the repentant sinner. But this time it was you who spoiled the play.'

'You remind me of a conjurer I once saw. He insisted on revealing all his tricks, nothing was allowed to be hidden from the audience. And so his performance was a complete failure.'

I have been doing my best not to drive too quickly, but even so, we have reached the airport. It is two hours before Diam's plane leaves. We sit down on a bench at the far end of one of the piers. It is windy, but the sun is shining.

Diam starts reading a magazine. I have a feeling that she doesn't want to see me in the role of the blubbering repentant sinner. I go down into the departure lounge to buy myself a paperback.

I have just got down there when I notice a girl with large breasts coming along dragging two suitcases (the girl, that is), the girl who was kind enough to lend me a bed last night.

We only exchange glances. She throws her suitcases up on a pair of scales, and is given a ticket, whereupon we both make for the toilet. I go ahead and am completely unconcerned that it says Ladies on the sign. She follows without hesitation. Once inside the little cubicle, we satisfy our common need, without undoing more buttons than absolutely necessary.

When we are both satisfied, we part without a word and go our separate ways. Only when we can scarcely see each other any longer does she smile her wry smile as a farewell.

I don't buy a paperback, but go straight back up to Diam.

'Diam, shouldn't we go back home and enjoy our last day together?'

She immediately puts down her magazine and gets up.

'Yes. We've got a day and a half left, of course.'

I'm amazed that it's been that easy.

'Why did you simply sit down and start reading, when you

140

really wanted to go home with me?'

'Why didn't you ask me?'

'It was as though there was something I had to get rid of first,' I admit.

'I know the feeling. I think I managed to unload in the car.'

We start to walk.

'Incidentally, you misunderstood me,' I say. 'It's quite right that I would rather write Marel's book than Lanson's. But I would far rather live Lanson's life than Marel's.'

She kisses me.

'And what can come of it if you first live Lanson's life, and then make the most of your having an imagination like Marel's?' she says.

We get into the car. I start laughing at myself.

'I actually didn't think you'd come with me. I think I've wasted a good deal of my powder.'

'Between ourselves, I can tell you why I am going with you: I'm collecting material; I want to write a book about my life with Alian Sandme.'

'So you had the last word after all.'

I hurry to kiss her and stop the movements of her lips that make it clear that she hasn't finished yet.

SALMIE

They have bound me. But quite gently so that I shan't discover it. There's a lot of paper, and a ball pen that I don't recognize. Perhaps my own has got lost.

The entire room is almost a sheet of white paper. With a black comma made up of my head and my arm. The bed, too, is white.

Sometimes Mea or Diam comes, I don't always have time to look. I must make a mental note of it next time. I think they've taken away some of my thoughts, because I had too many; for you can't think everything, it isn't good for you, not all at once. It gave me a pain in the head, but it's gone now.

There are some flowers, too, perhaps to tease me. They know perfectly well that I don't like them; when I touch a flower it unfolds in the shape of Diam.

They give me piles of paper. They call it some kind of therapy. Diam's eyes are looking down on me from the ceiling, I can see from them that what I'm writing is right. Sometimes they become sad in the middle of a sentence. Then, of course, I immediately stop.

It is part of the whole set-up that I must not know too much.

I once wrote, or wanted to write – I don't remember which – that every pain I suffer becomes one line in my collected works.

I can go on remembering lines I have written. It is as though they keep me together.

I've no more pain. You wouldn't think it could come from that little cut in my forehead. But of course, it comes more from inside and goes out. They are some rather nice pains they have in here, I can hardly feel them.

I wanted to write a book about a young man who thinks he is an old man remembering he was a young man. One of them was me. Only I can't remember how far I have got.

And then I can remember that Diam took the knife off me because she didn't want to cut me. She didn't know that I just wanted to show her how it hurt.

If I didn't write it all down, I wouldn't know how much of it I had thought and how much I still needed to think. Now I shall perhaps be thinking it twice, because their ball pens write more slowly. I'll get my own if only I tell them that my own writes more quickly.

I'm not trying at all to write quickly. I think now and then. They don't mind my thinking my own thoughts. It was some other people's thoughts they cut out.

If you only had a single thought left, it would have to be beautiful. Perhaps they haven't removed them all, because they keep on hurting me.

And I have written something about thoughts before. That's because my thoughts often want to decide what I am to write.

I know perfectly well that it's a hospital, they don't need to avoid telling me. And they often tell me, but even so, I know it perfectly well, beforehand.

They haven't told me how many pages I need to have written before I'm cured. Perhaps I'll be let out when there isn't any more paper left. Perhaps they'll come with some more paper.

I write less and less; then what I write looks pretty healthy. I can fool them in that way.

Sometimes I find it difficult to wait to write. Then I write. Sometimes I can wait. Then I write if the sentence seems to be healthy.

I wait for the thoughts. There are still a lot of them. But they differ from one another. I can choose. When I choose a 'healthy' sentence, I am a little healthier.

I can tell stories. When you tell stories, what you write is always right.

There's a man lying in my bed. That's my story. He's looking at the ceiling. His walls are white. His bed is white. He is ill.

I am well. I don't need to tell stories.

Diam looks straight into my eyes. She moves her lips without saying anything. I am telling a story. Diam's hair is waiting for my hand.

The man in my bed is ill. It's his fault I'm ill. I write the healthy sentences and become myself again. And stop being him.

Occasionally he makes me write something wrong. Because he is ill. It's on the brink all the time.

But now I can better write without thinking first. When I was well I suffered from having to think too much first, before I could write. Now I don't need to think.

I remember I could see lots of Diams. So many that I didn't know them all. They frightened me. I wanted to know them all. So I wanted to cut out those I didn't know. But the Diam I knew took the knife from me. I only cut myself a little.

I can remember that we spoke to each other. I can remember that I spoke more and more. When you speak you should also refrain from writing the sentences that don't look healthy. That's why I'm better now, because I can refrain.

There was suddenly supposed to be an entire pattern up in my head. There wasn't room for it. That was why I talked so much. They've cut it out. That's why I'm writing myself well. You write yourself well by cutting out the unwell.

SALMIN

I put my hand up to my head, and am a little frightened by the blood. I have a feeling that I must make an enormous exertion if I am to go on.

Diam seems dreadfully scared. She doesn't know what to do. I have sat down quietly. But she isn't sure how I am.

I look at the broken vase.

'It doesn't matter about that,' I say. 'I wasn't particularly fond of it in any case. And besides, I never have any flowers.'

Diam goes off with the knife. I deliberately don't turn round to see what she does with it.

'How do you feel, Alian?'

'I'm all right. But it's bleeding a bit.'

'Yes, lie down, and I'll try to stop it.'

It helps her that she's found something to do. She helps me over to the couch so I can lie down. She comes with water and some rags. I savour lying quite still with my eyes closed while she makes me comfortable. It takes a delightfully long time.

I carefully avoid touching her so as not to make her afraid of me, although it is difficult to keep my fingers to myself.

'There,' she says. 'It's all right now. No, you'd better stay lying down.'

'No, there's nothing wrong with me,' I say and sit up.

She starts tidying up, first takes the water away, and then the broken pieces of vase.

'Diam, I'd like to tell you what it was.'

The thought has crossed my mind that she might have misunderstood it all. Perhaps she has begun to feel sorry for me instead. Or perhaps she thinks I did it so that she should feel sorry for me. I shall have to tell her how it all hangs together.   'No, Alian, you don't need to talk about it. Perhaps it'll be best not to talk about it.'

'I only did it to warn you against me. I'm perfectly all right; you don't need to worry about anything. I just wanted, sort of, to warn you against me. I thought that if I pretended to have an attack like that, then you'd know a bit more about what I can be like. But, well, there's nothing at all wrong with me. If I don't quite feel up to a situation, it might happen now and again that I pretend to have an attack like that, or whatever we're to call it.'

'You don't need to talk about it so much. Everything's perfectly all right. And it wasn't my vase in any case.'

'I simply thought it my duty to warn you about me. If I can't trust myself, it would be foolish for you to.'

'What was it you couldn't cope with?'

'It was as if there was too much of you. I mean, I can't quite live up to you. I wanted to do something quite unique to show myself worthy of you, no, that's a silly word. So as to make a good impression on you. But of course, I couldn't think of anything good enough for you. And then I thought that if I pretended to go mad you'd realize I wasn't the right person for you.'

'I can't see the two things have anything to do with each other. And then you tell me about it all afterwards.'

'I realized that perhaps it hadn't had the intended effect. Perhaps you had felt sorry for me.'

'Perhaps I'm not allowed to do that, either?'

'But it would have been worse still if you thought that I'd done it all to make you feel sorry for me.'

'I really think you are best at being miserable,' she says. 'You are so used to missing me and being unhappy about it that when at last you've got me, you have to find something else to be miserable about.'

'You've probably got something there,' I say earnestly. I feel that perhaps we are about to get on to the right track after making a long detour together.

'I'm working on a great project. I'm going to write a big manual on how to become unhappy.'

'You must have plenty to base it on.'

'Yes. The main part of it will be made up of four large sections, of which the third is going to be about you: Setting yourself unattainable objectives, making unfulfillable demands.'

'Thank you. How flattering,' she says with a laugh. She comes over and sits down close to me, moves a tempting mouth in the direction of mine, and then draws back with a teasing smile.

My disappointed lips form the words: 'The motto of the book is to be: No day is lived without pain or without a hope that failed.'

SANDAL

This night is followed by many beautiful nights at the countess' home, although none of them can quite reach the heights of bliss of the first one. The countess frequently gives me access to her bedroom and even lets herself be seen in public together with me on several occasions. I adapt as best I can and take pride in the countess' friendship – and love, if I dare thus describe her feelings for me.

Although the relationship is perhaps not a hundred per cent satisfactory to me in every respect, it nevertheless comes as a shock when suddenly, one day, I discover that she has left without warning.

It is not difficult to trace the countess to New York, but further progress then becomes laborious indeed, even though by now I have acquired a highly-developed instinct for guessing where she is likely to be found.

Nor has she made the task easy for me this time. She has again renounced the title of countess, and is living as an ordinary housewife in one of the suburbs of New York, married to a perfectly ordinary man with a perfectly ordinary job.

She wears her hair in plaits and is dressed in perfectly ordinary clothes, though with just a little too much hint of fashion; but apart from that, she is unmistakably Diam.

But she is certainly no easier to win than when acting the countess. For a time my efforts seem to be quite hopeless when confronted with the narrow, constricting moral concepts which she has now acquired. I buy a house close by, and slowly I get a foot inside her door, for the simple reason that her quite ordinary husband and quite ordinary life in the quite ordinary house are beginning to bore her a little.

But once contact has finally been established, nothing is quite ordinary any more. Whereas Lowis was sophisticated, Jessap experienced and the countess distinguished, Diam is now, as my American housewife, so complicated and unfathomable that during our meetings I completely forget myself in my efforts to get through to her.

But of course, my good fortune does not last for ever. The day comes when once more I know the intense feeling of emptiness at having lost my Diam. And then, one day I experience the happiness of finding Diam again for the first time.

The most difficult situation I experience is when I discover her in the shape of a Japanese peasant girl. Our shortest association is in the interval when I track her down as a singer in Berlin.

One evening, I am sitting on a bench on a hillside in Algiers. From where I am sitting, far below me, I can see the garden in which is the Diam with whom I was united a short time ago, and whom I have only left in order to enjoy the cool of evening.

My eye happens to fall on one of my arms. It is soft and a little roundish, as though it has not been able to change and keep pace with me in the course of my indefatigable searches. But even as I look at it, it becomes more sinuous and hairy. Before my very eyes it shrivels up, the skin becomes wrinkled and turns pale. After a while, the veins become raised, and it starts shaking.

I can't stop this process, but can only be a passive observer. It is not the speed of it that frightens me, it is this slow, inexorable transformation, this sure path to annihilation.

It is obvious to me that there will soon be nothing left of the life I have spent looking for Diam. I feel a certain satisfaction in knowing that no more will she be disappearing for me, and that now it's my turn to be missed.

My strength fades. I lie down on the bench. I feel a profound joy at having met Diam so early in my life, at having been able to search for her so many times, at having found her in so many shapes, at so often having been able to feel her body against mine for the first time.

There is an orange tree above me, bearing both flowers and fruits. And above that again I can see a pair of Diam's eyes. I smile to them, and close mine.

SANDAT

The countess is infinitely beautiful as she lies in my arm, at my side, relaxed, filled with satisfaction after our love-making. Her slender, white, naked body, the hair spread out around her head, one lock of it lying on her shoulder and reaching out towards one of her breasts. Her smile that indicates that at this moment she belongs to me alone. Her one arm is resting on my side, cooling, and tempting me to renewed contact. Her eyelids are closed and quiver gently, her lips move a little and transform her smile as she senses my eyes fixed on her.

Diam remains quite still, letting me drink in every detail of her beauty, letting me take picture after picture to keep in the album of my memories. Her cheek with the beauty spot which I touch to make her smile.

At last I am so sated with visual impressions that I have to bend over her and thank her for them. My mouth finds hers, my lips are tightly pressed against hers, when there is a knock on the door. The countess starts. We remain in our comfortable position.

'Would you please open the door.'

Our tongues are the only things we can move without making a noise, and we make the most of that. The man outside takes hold of the door. It is locked.

'I know there's someone in there. Open up immediately.'

We stay lying there. We look in each other's eyes, we go on kissing each other, while waiting for the importunate fellow to go away.

The knocking becomes louder, someone is shaking the door. The man sounds furious.

'Is there anyone in there? Open up.'

Eventually he gives up, we can hear his footsteps as he goes down the long corridor.

'He sounded angry,' I say. 'Who could it be, I wonder? Surely we're entitled to be here?'

The countess tears herself away from me. I have the impression that she is suddenly frightened. I don't know what to believe.

'Suppose he comes back?' she says nervously.

'What should he come back for? The door's locked.'

I try to calm her by stroking her bare skin. It helps before long, and we begin once more to turn our attention to each other.

We have not heard footsteps. We hear a couple of violent blows on the door, which force it to give. The panelling isn't sufficient to withstand the pressure, a piece of boarding is pushed in, immediately followed by a hand that presses the handle down so that the door bursts open.

Two huge, angry men enter the room. Gallantly, I cover the countess over before myself.

One of the men is a waiter. The other is thick-set and bald, and looks as though he is used to giving orders.

'Ah, there you are,' he exclaims furiously.

I get up in all my towering strength, holding a handkerchief to cover my shame.

'What on earth is the idea?' I thunder as best I can without laughing.

The fat bald man stands there wriggling at the thought of having to direct his anger on himself.

'Yes, that's what *I'm* wondering,' he mumbles.

He looks round the untidy room, in the hope of catching sight of a dead body or some other unmistakable sign of a crime having been committed so that he can use it to justify his anger. All he catches sight of are the various articles of clothing, scattered about everywhere; apart from the countess' gown and beads they include a daring, shiny red dress and a stained smock.

'We thought something had happened,' he explains more and more humbly. 'You've not been outside the door for three days.'

'Do you mean to say,' I roar, agitating my handkerchief in the process. 'Are you saying that after having to pay through the nose for occupying the room for three days, we should have to show ourselves outside it?'

Diam has hidden her face in the pillow. The half-suffocated sounds coming from her don't make it any easier for me to keep a straight face.

'No, that's not what we mean. But it's not usual ... we were afraid that something had happened, an accident. There are so many people who try to buzz off, so even if this is the fourth floor you never know.'

'People had heard some curious noises, and then the hall porter had a feeling there was something suspicious, too ...' begins the waiter, but then realizes it would be wiser to stay silent.

'Well, we thought,' interrupts the bald man. 'You know, it's not usual just to live in the same place for three days without going out.'

'We've been all over the place,' I say, thinking warmly of the half-suffocated countess in the bed.

The fat man now makes to withdraw, he bows and presents his apologies; he is about to complain again, but thinks better of it, examines the door to see how much damage has been done, and finally disappears.

After this episode it is impossible to resume our play, but our time is also running out. We pack London, Paris and

Rome all together in the suitcase.

'Thank you, Countess,' I say and kiss her gratefully. 'That's the best life I've ever had.'

'You must thank Lowis and Jessap, too,' says the countess.

I express my profound admiration for these two, as well. We dress and go across to the smashed door so as to leave this world.

SANDEL

I install myself as comfortably as can be done in a bare hotel
room, switch on a lamp in a corner, find a stool for my legs
and settle down to work.

I am still occupied in this way when Diam arrives.

'Hi,' she says exuberantly. 'Oh, you look pretty comfortable.'

I wave to her and carry on reading. She has sat down on
the edge of the bed.

'Are you sulking?'

'No, of course not. Why do you think that?' I ask in
amazement.

'You're just sitting there without a word. Can't you be
bothered talking to me?'

'Yes, of course I can.'

I turn towards her to show willing. She comes across and
lays a hand on my head. She ruffles up my hair a little, lifts it
up to see how far my baldness has progressed.

'What do you think we should talk about?' I ask attentively.

'I don't know. What are you doing?'

'It's something for a book. Are you sure you can be
bothered hearing about it?'

'Yes,' she says, and seems genuinely keen.

'I don't mind telling you about it if you're really interested.'

'Yes, of course I am.'

'Iron Nihilsen is a big, fine man, equipped with a long
blond beard of the sort you really only find in wise men. He's
no wise man. But he is irreproachable in the way he attends to

155

his work in town, and he looks after his parents well. Until one day, as the result of an unfortunate idea, he loses his story.'

Diam has crossed her legs. One leg is swinging to and fro and is not far from reaching my legs. I settle down more comfortably and get further back into the chair.

'I've not yet quite decided how he's deprived of his story. Perhaps he meets some mysterious author who claims he's run out of inspiration and persuades Iron to sell him his story for a large sum of money. But with everything collapsing around him, Iron realizes what it means to have to do without his story. And things get worse of course when everyone else discovers that there's a story-less man in their midst. He is taunted and derided, pestered and teased wherever he turns up.'

Diam is taking off her stockings. She does so very slowly and meticulously. As she lifts up her dress to get hold of the top of them I can see her long, smooth legs in their whole extent. She gives me a friendly smile, perhaps to indicate that I can continue.

'Everything begins to go wrong for him. He loses his job – how can a firm employ a man without a story? He loses his friends – Who likes to be asked: What has this story-less friend of yours been doing recently? The last bond he loses is with his parents. First of all, his father gives up in the face of an impossible state of affairs. Not only does he disinherit his son, but he disowns him as a member of the family and has his name removed from the register of births. His mother is the last to let go of him. She rids herself of her memories of him, burns his baby shoes and his rocking horse and repudiates his children's games. She even goes so far as to start forgetting his name.'

Diam listens attentively while stretching, brushing her hair, inspecting herself in the mirror, and repairing her make-up, although I thought she was on her way to bed.

'Iron has nothing left to hold on to. No house will take him in, no job is open to him, no one will talk to him. Soon he has become so despised and rejected that no one will even stoop to point fingers at him, shout insults at him or spit on him.'

Diam is still pottering about, trying to disturb me as little as possible. She begins to take off her dress. Stands there for a moment with her dress over her head and her arms stretched up, in the position she knows I find it difficult to resist. She wriggles her body to make her dress fall of its own accord. When she has succeeded, she is standing before me in her bra and panties. She absent-mindedly strokes her skin with her hands while listening attentively to me.

'Late one evening, as Iron is wandering the streets with nowhere to go, he suddenly becomes aware of a house he hasn't seen before. He knows the street well and has often passed the house on the right and the house on the left, but this house is completely new to him. Baffled, for houses don't just appear in the course of a day, he turns around to see whether after all he has mistaken the place. The street is exactly what he has been expecting, but when he turns round again, the house has vanished once more.'

Diam is standing just in front of me, with her side turned towards me. She undoes her bra and takes it off. She remains standing there. The profile of her breasts is almost directly in front of my eyes. She turns towards me and stretches over me to take something off the shelf behind my chair. She has to take a step closer to reach it. Her breasts are immediately in front of my lips.

'Iron thinks deeply about this happening. He is enfeebled and realizes that the house must have resulted from a momentary feverish fantasy. And so he trudges on without doing any more about it.'

Diam has taken some cream off the shelf. She throws the tube on to the bed. Again she is standing immediately in front of me. She takes off her briefs. Very slowly and meticulously, it seems to me. Having discarded them, she performs a couple of gymnastic movements to enjoy the freedom of her body.

'And yet Iron can't get this experience out of his mind. Time and time again his thoughts return to this vision that seemed so real to him, even if it was unusual. So before long, he retraces his steps to the same place. He's both amazed and relieved to discover that the house is now there again. He wants to summon other people as witnesses, and looks up and down the street, which is completely deserted. The house has vanished when he turns back towards it again.'

Diam has taken a little cream on her fingers and started to rub her back with it. She has to stretch in order to cover it all.

'This time he doesn't go very far away from the spot, and then only immediately to hurry back. The house is there, and without giving it time to disappear he rushes in through the door. Inside, it is dark and gloomy. He has to grope his way forward, and discovers that there is no ground floor, let alone one above it. The only way in leads down into what one would normally call a cellar.'

Now Diam is rubbing cream on her legs. She puts her foot on the arm of my chair so that I have to move my arm to make room for her. First one leg, meticulously, then the other.

'The cellar is only dimly lit, but a large number of people are gathered there. Shy as he has become by now, Iron finds a corner where he sits down unnoticed. It is obvious to him that the place is a pub, though a somewhat unusual one. The landlord comes and offers him a drink, without asking any questions. Now Iron has time to look around. The strangest people are sitting there all on their own, drinking, walking to and fro alone, talking to themselves, stealing along the damp walls. One man is walking back and forth near a mirror on the wall, wanting to look in it, but each time thinking better of it and hurrying away. One man is walking around backwards, with his eyes fixed all the time on the ground behind him. Another is addressing himself to a corner and seems distressed on not receiving any answer. One man is walking around holding his hand to his face all the time. Behind him walks a little shrimp of a man who steals across to the mirror when it is free, but immediately puts his hand to his face when he reaches it.'

Diam laughs, more heartily than my story gives occasion for. She has finished rubbing in cream on her front. She lies down on the bed, just opposite me.

'A dog has come into the room, it sniffs around and suddenly collides with a man. Someone at the side of Iron leans forward and explains in a kindly voice: "That man is without a smell, so the dog hadn't noticed him."'

This man talking to him has placed a screen between himself and the light on the table. – "My name is Schlemihl", he says. "I don't have a shadow. I suppose you'd like to be told what's going on? The man by the mirror is called Spikher, he has no reflection. He gave it to a girl who claimed she loved him deeply. Oh, never mind the names, you can't remember them in any case. The man going backwards and looking at the ground leaves no traces. It's just the same if he walks in snow or soft earth, he has been condemned to disappear without trace. The man hiding his face has no nose. The little one behind him has a nose all right, and he has a reflection, too. But his reflection has no nose. The man in the corner has given his echo to a girl who was enamoured of his voice. The place and the landlord have no name."'

Diam is lying on her back, relaxing, with her arms and legs

spread out.

'The man beside Iron falls silent and looks at him intently. – "So what has brought you here?" he asks. Several others in the room have drawn closer to hear the reply from their new fellow-sufferer. Iron Nihilsen feels secure among all these people who are just as unhappy as he, and he replies, as is true, that he has no story. An amazed murmur is heard from the others, all of whom are now gathered around his table. Outraged, the man without a nose exclaims: "But everyone must have a story.'

And the outrage spreads among this assemblage of unusual people. A mood of opposition gathers towards poor Iron. But suddenly a change comes over them. "Hey," one of them shouts. "Listen to me, you can have mine, I've got far too much."'

Diam rolls over, turning a smooth, round backside towards me. She has closed her eyes.

'And straight away another one calls out and offers his story, and a third and a fourth. For all have realized that their problem is precisely that they have rather more of a story than they like. Iron is overwhelmed with offers and can hardly avoid having *one* forced on him. He is not left in peace until he has promised to take over a story from one of those present, but he wants time to choose.

He is now permitted to walk around the rooms, for in the adjoining rooms, too, there are people with problems of a similar nature.'

Diam has started to breathe deeply. Luckily, she can't see that I am smiling triumphantly. Her fair, lithe body lies spread out before me.

'Finally, Iron meets a girl with whom he falls in love on the spot, and who promises to help him out of his difficulties. She is called Maid, and is a girl without shame. Now, this woman leads Iron through all kinds of torments and disappointments. She lets him down and cheats him in every conceivable manner. She constantly stokes his infatuation and exploits it daily in order to inflict ever new and worse suffering on him. She humiliates him, ridicules him, scorns him, affronts his love. Until Iron is equipped with a full complement of disappointments and sorrows and bewails the fact that he has received his story of suffering.'

I sit still for a moment to be sure that Diam is asleep. I quietly undress, now that no one can see the effect her striptease act has had on me. Then, I gently lay a blanket over her, put out the light and lie down.

Before falling asleep, I can't resist the temptation to whisper:

'There you can see for yourself that I could be bothered to talk to you.'

At that moment an unexpected hand feels its way in between my legs.

'If you're not sulking, then perhaps you can be bothered to touch me as much?'

SANDES

On the way home I get the taxi to stop at a department store that is open. I buy a bra, a fairly large size, and a bottle of perfume.

When I get home I first of all lie down in the bed. As a result it looks fairly untidy. I make a rather clumsy show of smoothing down the mess. I put the bra under the pillow and sprinkle just a tiny drop of perfume around – she has a uniquely fine sense of smell – and hide the bottle.

When Diam finally steals in and gently opens the door – she probably hopes I'm asleep so she can get into bed unnoticed – I am by complete coincidence lying comfortably on the bed with my back to the door, speaking on the telephone. I don't notice her. I mention my private telephone number.

'Yes, my dear,' I say gently. 'Do give me a ring, and we'll work something out ... Yes, that would be lovely. Fine, goodbye and – thank you.'

That last word is given all the sweetness and intensity that my voice can mobilize. When I put down the phone, Diam comes in properly.

'Oh, I thought you were asleep,' she says, opening the door wide.

I am not embarrassed at being caught in the act of phoning, that would be exaggerating things, and I don't try to explain anything away.

She sniffs the air, but so slightly that I have no reason to notice it. She sits down on her bed, tidies the pillow and finds the wretched article of clothing.

'What's that,' she says, betraying no particular interest and allowing it to dangle from the end of one finger.

'It's your bra,' I say indifferently.

'No.'

'But it must be, how should it have got there otherwise?'

I am not upset when she doesn't believe me, simply stubborn.

'But surely you can see it doesn't fit me,' she says, blushing a little.

'Is it really not yours? Then it must have been left here by the people before us ... Oh, that's really too bad; it means they haven't changed the bedclothes since ... They can't do that.'

I have already grabbed the telephone to ring down and complain. She is tired of hearing me make so much out of an unsuccessful lie.

'No, then it must be one of mine after all,' she says. 'Anyhow, I only came to fetch my things. I'm off again. Just you sleep on.'

And sure enough, she gathers her belongings, gives me a good night kiss, and goes.

The following morning we happen to meet in the restaurant downstairs over breakfast. She doesn't look as though she has had much sleep during the night, but of course they only had such a short time together. I haven't slept much, either, for I was taken up with an exciting book.

'Has Hune left?' I ask casually.

She nods, her mouth full of bread. Her bag is at her feet.

'I'm afraid I'm going to have to go home,' I say. 'It's a shame, but...'

'That suits me fine,' she interrupts me. 'I'll go on down south. Doria can't stand in for me any longer.'

We take leave of each other. Even kiss each other goodbye.

After another couple of days we are both at home with our families. Living so relatively close to each other and having so

163

many mutual acquaintances as we do, does pose a few problems for us.

On one of the first days, in order to avoid coming across her, I prefer to put a note in the place where we used to leave messages for each other. On my slip of paper I draw her attention to the fact that I have been invited that evening to visit one of our mutual friends, I hope she will be so considerate as to stay away so that I shan't be compelled to be in her company.

The note doesn't have the hoped-for effect, on the contrary, Diam is so vengeful and bitter that she comes and ruins my evening.

So when there is a message from her a couple of days later to the effect that that evening she has thought of going to a theatre première, and that she hopes that I will be sufficiently understanding to stay away, I find it reasonable to take my revenge by going to this première in which I was not otherwise particularly interested.

A veritable war breaks out between us to see who can most often get in the other's way. If I leave a message telling her that the following afternoon I have thought of going for a walk in the park between three and four, I can be almost sure of finding Diam at the park entrance, waiting there with the undisguised intention of spoiling my walk. But if she has left a message to the effect that the following day she has thought of going to look at dresses in such and such a shop at such and such a time, I naturally do not neglect this opportunity to get my own back for her harassment.

So far she has not been bold enough to go so far in her malicious behaviour as to speak to me, but I have a feeling she is planning to do so, for which reason, in order to anticipate her malicious plans, the next time we meet in the park I go straight across to her and say: 'We had quite a nice time together, thank you.'

She stops, dumbfounded.

'Yes, thank *you*,' she replies sarcastically.

Her reply stings me and I try to think up some devastating remark.

'I hope you enjoyed it,' I say, although I am not entirely satisfied with the force in this phrase.

'No-o,' she says. 'But you obviously did.'

I laugh scornfully until I start to think about her words.

'You didn't actually give me the chance to enjoy all that much,' I say rather passively.

'Incidentally, I happened to take your girlfriend's bra with me.'

'Oh, you can keep that. It was one I had just bought.'

She looks at me in amazement.

'I hope you *slept* well,' I hasten to say in order to make the most of her surprise.

'I didn't sleep at all,' she says honestly. 'It was a miserable room they gave me.'

'But I thought that Hune ...'

'Hune had already left in the evening.'

I am beginning to have a feeling that it is more important to get to the bottom of all this than to retail further spiteful remarks.

'You were being foolish, so I took a room for myself,' she admits.

'You were being foolish, so I bought a bra and pretended I was ringing someone.'

'You were being foolish, so I got Hune to invite me out.'

'What on earth had I done?'

'What did you do for the two hours you said you were parking the car?'

'I simply parked it, bought a suitcase and something to put

in it, and made my way up to you.'

This leaves me feeling a bit of a fool.

'I'm thinking of going down to the cottage,' I say. 'That's really what I wanted to say.'

'I'll soon be going south again. The night train stops for twelve minutes. I hope you'll make sure you're not there.'

'We'll see,' I reply. 'I'll probably not be there.'

'No, obviously.'

SANGEN

T he third day with Diam turns into an unbroken chain of beautiful moments.

Diam, turning in her sleep, her eyes closed, and adopting a position like a graceful sculpture of living flesh.

Diam, naked, leaning forward to find her shoes.

Diam, with her foot on my knee while she arranges her stocking.

Diam, with her head on one side so that her newly brushed hair cascades down.

Diam, with a little pensive smile, leaning against the side of the lift.

Diam, leaping down from the hotel steps into my embrace.

Diam's calves, their gliding movements framed by the undulating hem of her dress.

Diam, her lips parted in an exclamation, turning around so suddenly that her hair only follows slowly after her.

I collect her calmly and carefully like a collector who has made a substantial discovery and is now registering its individual components with a pounding heart. I blissfully accept the constant stream of beauty emanating from her.

Diam's eyes looking at me as she is about to alight from the taxi.

Diam's mouth and the lines on her forehead as she sits wondering what we should have to eat.

I observe her in admiration, I listen happily to what she has to tell me. I whisper little nothings to her, and watch her smiling at them all.

Diam's lips as she tries to cope with the spaghetti.

Diam's hands as they teach me a new method.

I am so taken with her that I can't refrain from touching her. And when I have once started touching her, it is difficult to stop.

Diam's slender shoulders moving beneath my hand.

Diam's hand quietly waiting for my finger to trace its entire outline.

Diam's cheek that is so infinitely soft beneath my fingers.

I fix her remarks in my mind so as to be able to hear them again and again. I carefully note the intonation, the laughter, the tiny pauses.

Diam saying: 'They've gone like a dream.'

Diam tossing her hair and saying: 'It'll be strange to have to do without you again, not just to have you when I stretch out my hand.'

Diam with a placatory smile before saying, 'Now I won't be seeing you for a while.'

I fill her glass. We drink rather a lot so as to be so happy that we don't discover how miserable we ought to be.

Diam putting her hand in mine.

Diam laughing as I turn her head to admire her profile.

I have a feeling gnawing slowly at me. I have not wanted to let it develop, because time is so short after all. A feeling that everything is perhaps not as it ought to be.

Has Diam enjoyed our time together? Been happy in the same way as I?

I try to banish the thought. But I am very intoxicated, and she is going to leave very soon. I must have an answer to this question before it's too late.

Have I done it all wrong? Have I simply exploited Diam? I have absorbed impressions, I have extracted moments of experience from her. I have put her on a pedestal and walked around her to satisfy my yearning for beauty, I have turned her round, turned her face so as to get it in the most beautiful positions and see her from the most attractive angles.

Diam continuing eating and looking around the room.

I have used her without seeking to give her anything. I am afraid I am beginning to understand far too much.

Diam dries her lips.

I don't know how she feels. I simply see her, just as I have all the time simply seen her, without knowing anything about her. I understand how it might have happened: Diam has been happy for my interest, flattered by my attentions, satisfied with the brief meetings we could arrange, during which I could express my admiration. But I have pressed her further than she herself had been expecting, have pressed her to go through with this meeting. She is kind, doesn't want to upset me, is afraid I might feel hurt. And so she accepts this rendezvous, takes part in it for my sake. And I extract beauty from her, ensure experiences with her, in the belief that she too is content with this.

I understand that I have to give her a possibility of extracting herself from the relationship. I don't want to go on against her wishes. But I know she will not say it of her own accord. I must give her a chance.

There is so little time left. I have paid the bill. We can only just make the train.

It will be difficult to have to break off contact with her, but it is worse to go on with the insight I now have.

'Diam,' I say hesitantly. 'Now we'll once more only be able to meet occasionally for a few minutes.'

She nods.

'I understand if you don't get much out of that. Diam, I would awfully like to go on meeting you. But I don't really want to if you don't.'

She looks at me for a long time. Slowly, she nods.

'Is that your way of saying we must stop?'

169

I can see she is upset. I feel almost certain she is upset. I know a bit about what she is feeling. That is enough.

'No,' I am so agitated I almost shout. 'No, it's not me who wants to stop. I was merely afraid that that's what you wanted.'

'Silly chap,' she says before I kiss her.

I know what she feels as we walk close to each other on our way to the train. I see her climb into it, I see the train leave. I am sad, but I think I know something of what she is feeling. That is the most important thing.

When the train has disappeared a strange doubt creeps over me.

SANGER

'Why do you like me?' she asks, and her words wake me up.

'I'll tell you,' I say sleepily, and try to find myself, or at least a little portion of me. – 'My ideal woman is short and plump, with short dark hair, not too pretty, but enormously considerate, so that she always leaves me to have a lie in in a morning. The reason why I like you, for I think I do, is that in certain respects you differ from my ideal. Wouldn't it perhaps be rather dull if you had formed an image of an ideal girl, and then she turned up and couldn't add anything new to the image? I find it stimulating that you yourself are an irrefutable argument in favour of fair hair being superior to dark, and so on. In that way you renew me. And that's good for me.'

'I love big silent men.'

'Well, I'm not all that small.'

She gives me an appraising look and laughs.

And we sit on a bench looking at the fountain.

'Two and a half days, and I still don't understand you,' she says despondently.

'Thank you. I'll tell you how I've fooled you. I'm not at all the person you were talking to yesterday. I have a little switch in here. Like everyone else, I'm filled with an urge not to be myself, to break out of myself, or at least to turn my back on myself, and I've made a habit of doing that as often as possible.

'I suppose now I'd better ask you: Don't you think you'd better produce some illustration to this profound and epoch-making idea?'

'All right, as you seem to be so preoccupied with the

171

question. When I was young I read somewhere that girls actually like a certain shyness in young men. And so I affected a certain shyness. Turned myself into a shy young man. In my youth, when my shyness probably suited me, that resulted in my not making contact with girls. And now that I'm no longer young, I can certainly make contact with them, but shyness is no longer fitting: on the contrary it is inclined to get rather a lot in the way. So my shyness seems to have been misdirected. What do I do, then? Get rid of it. I can't, it's become so deeply rooted, it's really part of me by now. But I force myself out of myself. I become two different beings: the shy man and the experienced man who has chosen to feign shyness.'

'Either the shy man or the experienced man is expressing himself badly, I don't understand what he's saying,' says Diam, shaking her head.

And we are in the museum, looking at a picture that doesn't interest us.

'Of course,' says the Diam standing with her back to the painting. 'I have really always had a happy and uncomplicated disposition.'

'Of course,' says the Diam standing facing the painting. 'I'm a mournful sort of person, full of doubts and rather melancholy.'

'I know the feeling,' I say, frowning and deflated. 'I've always been thoughtful and a little otherworldly.'

'What am I saying?' I shout in order to drown my own voice, elegantly swinging myself up to the top of an enormous statue, and beating my breast. 'Always ready for a joke – I've never refused to take part in a sporting competition.'

'I have a deep-seated urge to help others and be self-sacrificing,' Diam shouts up to me. 'Come down now before you hurt yourself.'

'I'm very self-reliant and want to be independent,' shouts Diam. Absorbed by the picture though I am, she takes me by the arm and drags me along with her. 'Come on, we're going now, you've been standing there long enough.'

And we go off for a swim in the big public pool.

'Because I'm so shy,' I say bluntly, 'I must know a girl for thirty-four years, or eight or eleven, before I dare touch her. Before that I don't feel I know her well enough to be able to risk it. Until then, I don't know what she's thinking, or what she's like, you know.'

I touch Diam's smooth, wet body. She splashes water in my face.

'I'll never learn to understand women,' I say, letting go of her. 'When after all these years I do finally touch you, it's not surprising that I persist.'

She swims across and kisses me. Then she splashes more water at me.

And we walk past shop windows with mirrors that reflect multiple versions of us.

'I want to know everything about you,' I say.

'I'm a quiet, respectable girl who likes to be your dream girl. And I'm an experienced woman who finds it relatively easy to make conquests and relatively difficult to say no.'

'No, you mustn't say that,' I exclaim, putting my hands to my ears.

And we arrive at the train, dejected and happy.

'We're not going to part,' I say. 'On the contrary, from now on we are going to be together in two different places. My mind will accompany your body in the train. It won't cease to look at you. To look at your beautiful legs as you change in your couchette, to look at your breasts when you stretch in the early morning. Not for one moment will you be out of my sight. At the same time, *your* thoughts will be with my body. Here, my body will go for walks in the streets while my lips carry on long conversations with your thoughts.'

Once more my lips kiss hers. Once more, her awareness allows itself to bask in my admiration.

My hand waves to hers. My thoughts become more and more distant. Her thoughts have fixed themselves in me.

SANGUD

And yet I wish from the bottom of my heart.

When I open my eyes Diam has grown younger. There is a quite young Diam standing in the train, ten years younger than when I closed them. Confused, I raise my hands to rub my eyes and see that my hands, too, have grown younger, I feel my cheeks, my hair. I, too, have grown young, quite a young man.

I don't understand what has happened.

But the train has come to a standstill, and the girl jumps out of it and rushes into my arms.

I begin to remember this young body, and my young, clumsy arms.

'Hello, Alian,' she cried exuberantly. 'I've been looking forward to seeing you.'

And slowly I am able to make this reality my own. I understand that I have dreamt a long dream in which Diam and I had become older. I imagined in vivid detail that we as grown people had a complicated tryst, made the more difficult by the fact that we were each married.

So vivid has my fantasy been that I can still not quite feel myself as the young man I am. Rather, I am a young man imagining himself to be an older man dreaming he is young.

We kiss. We have done that before, but not so fervently as now.

I have been standing lost in thought for so long while waiting for the train that I suddenly discover I am cold.

'Shall I take your case?'

She nods as though it were the most natural thing in the world. It is heavy. She strides off down the platform without turning round, and I hurry after her. Her dress swirls up and shows her legs.

The train leaves. A man is standing there, looking at his empty hands. He glances at us and seems to be about to burst into tears. Perhaps he's ill, or drunk.

Then we walk down the road, talking to each other. And Diam looks at clothes in the shop windows. We notice a magnificent blouse that I am on the point of asking whether I should buy for her. But I don't really dare, it could be that she'll think I'm not happy with the clothes she's wearing. And I most certainly am.

She is so beautiful that most people turn round to look at her. I walk beside her and pretend it's the most natural thing in the world. It isn't, when you're carrying such a heavy suitcase.

It's a relief when I think of suggesting that we should sit down on a bench in a park. I haven't the slightest idea of what I'm going to say to her, but luckily, she starts to tell me about something that happened in the train.

She asks why I am wearing such a big pair of sunglasses, and takes them off. I want to kiss her when she laughs at me, but I'm not sure she would like that.

I begin to explain something to her about the light and my eyes, and I sit blinking. Then I, too, start laughing and say that I think they look good.

When I am wearing them, I can better sit and look at her without her noticing it.

I fetch us each an ice cream. We stay on the bench and talk about the people walking past. I suddenly remember that probably I ought to have had a present for her, a bunch of flowers or something of the sort. Then I have an idea. With a matter-of-fact gesture I take out my ball pen and say: 'I'd like to give you this for coming.'

She is obviously pleased with it, or at least pretends she is. She thanks me and says she'll keep it. I can't persuade myself to tell her that it's almost finished. I'm sure she'll discover that at some stage.

I have a feeling that there is such a terrible lot of things we can do, there are so many things I would like to do together with her. But on consideration I can't think of anything, so we simply sit there talking. I like that, too, but I'm a little afraid she might find it boring. But I think it would be a bit too ordinary to go to the cinema. We've been there before, too, and this day ought to be something special.

Luckily she doesn't seem concerned and talks about all kinds of things. And before long I, too, start telling her some story. So somehow or other we while away the afternoon sitting on a bench, walking through the park with the heavy suitcase, and walking the streets. And we go into a shop and try on various things. We don't buy anything, but I see her in some new clothes. She is very smart, and then I shake my head and say, 'No, that's not exactly right for you. It doesn't suit your complexion.' Or: 'Doesn't it look a bit old fashioned?'

The shop assistant hurries to get something else out and maintains that this is the very latest thing, but we are extremely choosy and refuse everything. Diam winks at me, so often that I am almost afraid the assistant has noticed it, for she suddenly stops being all that keen to assist. But of course it might be because she has got tired of us.

Then we start chatting about what else we could try. Without intending doing it, of course. We could go in and say we wanted to buy a car, people do that so often in films. Or we could hire a dinner suit and a long gown – and not pay the hire charges, of course – and then pretend we were a distinguished couple, the count and countess, or something like that.

As we talk about these things I come to think of the dream I had while waiting for the train.

At last we are tired of wandering up and down the streets. I put the suitcase down, and we look around.

'What shall we do now?'

'We'll go and eat,' I say in just the right voice.

'Are you mad? We can't afford to,' she says, luckily.

'Well, we'd manage somehow, I suppose.'

We passed a restaurant a short while ago. We go back to it. It is an enormously posh place with lots of distinguished people. But the waiter who shows us to a table doesn't look askance at us. Otherwise, I am quite ready to make a fuss if he says anything.

The tables are antique, if not older, and everything people are eating looks dreadfully expensive. I can't help wondering whether I've got enough money, although I have decided beforehand not to start facing myself with that kind of problem.

We are given a menu and make our choices. Diam wants a lemonade with hers, and so I take one, too. People around us are having plenty to drink, though. There's someone dancing on the floor. There's a man clutching a woman so tight that I almost feel it is indecent. But of course, they're at an age when they think they can take any liberty they want. Luckily, Diam doesn't notice them.

'What are you doing with yourself nowadays?' she asks.

She knows perfectly well that I spend most of the day in my room without doing anything at all. She makes no comment, but she probably thinks I ought to set about something or other, either study or get a job.

'I've just written a poem,' I say so as to avoid a direct reply. 'About you.'

'Really? Have you got it with you, or do you know it by

heart?'

'No, I can't remember it. It's not particularly good in any case. About your hair and your eyes. But it's like the poems everyone else writes.'

'Even so, I'm glad you've been writing about me.'

'Well, you've got to write about someone, you can't just write poems about nothing at all.'

We eat slowly in order to spend as long as possible in the restaurant. On several occasions I feel an urge to kiss her, but I'm not sure whether she would like it, particularly not in such a place.

But I put my hand on hers, and she doesn't pull hers away. She looks thoughtful, I'd like to know what she's thinking.

'You look rather nice in that dress, actually,' I happen to say, because there are so many drunken people around me.

That produces no result, so I go on: 'I wouldn't mind making a film about you.'

It's strange how high you can get on a single lemonade.

'I've thought of becoming a naturalist,' I say without smiling. 'I want to study insects, and then I hope to be able to find a new species of ant that I'll call after you.'

She's not with me yet, she simply looks at me in surprise. Of course I have prepared this before leaving home. She is pretty good at English and knows perfectly well what an ant is:

'Can't you see how splendid it would look in an English encyclopedia: Diamant.'

She laughs so loud that she makes a man turn round and stare at us. I have a feeling that he is wishing he were in my place. And the dream from the platform turns up again.

I snatch the ball pen I have just given Diam; it's sticking out of her bag on the floor. Now, of course, I have revealed that I play with her name in my room at home, so I write on her serviette: My Diam. Then I alter the i a little to make it say My Dream.

SANGUR

I would give anything to be able to live together with Diam. But I open my eyes again. Both she and I know that we can't start our lives all over again. Time has made such a mark on us that it wouldn't work.

The train leaves. My spot of orange light disappears. My hands are infinitely empty.

I don't feel able to drive. I walk down one of the streets. My nerve system is paralysed, my senses are not functioning. Or perhaps it is just my brain that has received a shock.

Diam's feet are not walking in time with mine on the ground. Her hand doesn't worm its way down to mine in my trouser pocket. A puff of wind comes along, but it doesn't blow Diam's hair about.

The reflections in the shop windows show an gigantic void walking at my side. I don't increase my speed, I don't stop, there is no method by which I can get rid of this phantom.

No sudden burst of laughter comes cascading towards me from Diam. There is no hand to give mine an encouraging squeeze. I can go on endlessly without one of Diam's little remarks to amuse me.

There is nothing. There are no possibilities. I can't bear going on in this way, in this vacuum. I can't bear driving home to the empty cottage where all hope of life is far removed. I can't bear to go in anywhere and see people who are not Diam and listen to people without Diam hearing the same thing.

Nevertheless, I finish up near the car. There is no Diam to help in.

I drive slowly. Diam doesn't interfere with my driving. I drive backwards for a time in the belief that it will give vent to my desperation. Diam doesn't say I'm being too foolish.

The cottage smells of the lack of Diam. A depression in the cushions shows that they are missing Diam's body. Diam's absence is everywhere.

There is a piece of yawning empty paper. There is a lifeless ball pen. There is no other word but Diam. I don't need to write it, I remember it all too well. My lonely hand starts drawing. It tries to recreate the features it has felt so many times. Diam's face appears on the paper. The ball pen follows her outline. It turns into the first real likeness I have ever managed to draw.

I can't stay in the cottage where the silence gives echoes. The phantom draws me down to the beach. A rowing boat is there, in the shelter of which Diam and I have lain. There is no one there. No one will miss the boat. I loosen the rope, push the boat out into the water, and crawl up into it. I fix the oars and start to row out.

With an immense effort I realize that there is only one solution to this condition. I must allow my imagination to fill the void in order to endure it.

I picture Diam to myself, and that immediately makes my pain the greater. I have her tied and bound to the seat in the boat, I'm about to abduct her. She's freed. We are fleeing together. We are rowing out together to an eternal life at the other side of the ocean.

It's no good. I know I'm only fantasizing.

I imagine that Diam and I have overcome the external difficulties, that we have found a way of living together, for the rest of our lives. I am hoping that my wayward imagination will straight away come into play and tell me how miserable we shall be together, how we'll get on each other's nerves, different as we are, how we'll be bored, alike as we are. But the only thing my imagination produces is picture after picture of

Diam as I have seen her over the last three days.

I take the picture I have drawn and put it in the water and watch it begin to drift away, but soon it starts to sink.

I row back. I've made up my mind to go home and write an impassioned letter. To tell her that I can't stand it, that I can't do without her. Despite all our agreements, we must put our relationship on a more permanent basis. Now my imagination is more at home. The first plausible arguments appear. I feel a self-confident conviction that I'll be able to tempt her, be able to win her, if only I can formulate my letter sufficiently well. Perhaps not with a single letter. But I'll write torrents of letters. I can send her a letter every day. Formulated so thrillingly that she can't refrain from reading them. Perhaps the wisest thing will be not to proceed too directly. The first letter, the first letters, must not reveal my intention. They must only express my gratitude for these days. The next ones must strengthen the attack. Gradually she must be caught in a net of words from which she can't escape, a floodgate that will sweep her to me.

I pull the boat ashore and go home to the cottage.

It will be a long letter. I must lay bare my entire situation; only by speaking to her in total honesty do I have any chance of convincing her, she will immediately see through hollow attempts at persuasion, through all false flattery.

The essence of my series of letters will be these three days we have spent together.

When I am sitting in the cottage with the first piece of paper before me, the difficulties become plain. The entire task must be carefully planned. Already at this point I realize that the series of letters will be just as comprehensive as a whole novel, and that it will demand an equally strict composition. Nevertheless, I can't help starting on the first letter.

Dear Diam, I write, because the impression conveyed must

be quite relaxed, not artificially personal, not plucking at the heartstrings.

I continue: I had a strange experience when I arrived home in the cottage. After taking you to the train. After seeing it disappear with you. After driving home alone.

But now I realize I have got going quickly. This letter I've started on mustn't be the first. It must be prepared for, I must build up to it so that it can have the desired effect.

I take a large pile of white sheets and place them before me.

STOLEN

P eople.
There is a huge, empty world. In places the terrain is uneven, with hills and ravines. Elsewhere there are great flat stretches. There are areas that are yellow, there are vast green areas. There are red cliffs and there are vast oceans. Everywhere there is a void.

Between an ocean and a forest there is a long, white patch, a shoreline, a great stretch of white. There is a single black dot that is not moving. And far away from it there is another black dot that is moving, down towards the blue area. The dot is a man. He reaches the ocean and stops. He divides into two. The two men walk in opposite directions, along the waterline.

One of them stops at a boat. He divides. One of him drags the boat out into the water and sails off. The other walks up towards a cottage.

The other man walks along the ocean. He divides, and one of him walks up towards the forest while the other continues along the waterline.

One sails out in the boat. He divides. One of him sails on, the other sails back towards the shore.

The other one goes up towards the cottage. He divides. One of him goes into the cottage, the other takes a car and drives in the direction of the town.

One of them goes up towards the forest. He divides. One of him sits down on the forest floor, the other walks towards the cottage.

The other one reaches the other dot. It's a woman. He stops in surprise. They divide. They remain together, and they walk along the shore together.

They stay where they are and kiss. They divide. They part, and they walk together in a tight embrace towards a cottage.

They walk along the beach together. They divide. They go up and get into a car together, and they sit down together in the shelter of a rowing boat.

He searches for her. He divides. He finds her in a house, and he meets another walking along the beach.

Many of them reach the town at the same time. They divide. They throng everywhere. They go into a big house together. They go separately into a big house, she first and he later.

They search for each other. They go out into the forest and stop at a stream. They walk together and meet some they have just parted from.

They meet each other at a train. They divide. They become a young couple and an older couple. They go to a train and separate from each other. They hold around each other. They constantly divide. They go in and eat together, and the others go in and eat together. One couple laughs, the other quarrels.

They station themselves behind the counter in a shop. One of them takes an aeroplane. The other follows in an aeroplane. They divide. They populate new towns, more and more of them. They take trains.

They go into a shop and buy from those standing in the shop. They divide. They clothe themselves differently. They change names. They laugh.

They pursue each other, they sit on a bench, they write stories about each other, they smile to each other. They all divide.

They collide. He picks her up. They change. One lies down on the ground and dies. Some people bury him. Some people hide his body.

They are everywhere. They throng everywhere. They do

things. They speak. They writhe in agony. They hide their heads in their hands. One crawls along the ground.

They don't recognize each other even though they stem from the same two dots that started dividing. One hits out at another. Two embrace each other and try to become fused. They divide. One couple succeeds in becoming fused.

They can't see the pattern they form. All the time there are some laughing, all the time there are some jumping over a hedge. There is one smashing a vase. There is one giving him a kiss.

There are so many of them that all the time there is someone driving into a tree. There are many coming on a train, there are many boarding the train.

The pattern is visible, they can't avoid it, but they can't see it for themselves. One falls, another takes his place. There is a host making for the town, but there are also many making away from the town. There are some who know each other. There are always some passing each other in the pattern without seeing each other.

There is one who knocks against a door. He divides. One goes in one direction, the other in the other. One believes he is the only one going in one direction. The other believes he is the only one going in the other direction.

The green areas are swarming with dots, there are swarms of dots on the red areas, there are great swarms of dots going out to sea together.

Each of the dots denotes a little line in the pattern. None of them can see the line they denote, none of them can see the pattern which these lines make up together.

STOLER

M ankind.
There is a throng of beings moving in and out among each other. Apparently moving inexplicably and spasmodically.

One of them pushes his way forward among many others. He reaches the door. She is standing in the doorway.

He raises his hand and lets it slip through her hair. He is frightened at his action, and happy that he pulled himself together enough to carry it out.

She turns towards him. Delighted, he sees that she is not angry.

He draws her closer to him and they kiss. He feels quite confused at the many feelings flowing through him.

Her lips are soft, she returns his kiss. He is so entirely absorbed in this moment; he makes no attempt to understand it properly, or to recognize all the feelings stirring within him.

He takes her hand, and they start walking down towards the shore. Amazed, he thinks that this is the same hand he was sitting admiring just before.

He gives her hand a squeeze. His thoughts become almost confused when she turns her face towards him and smiles.

Once more, he lets his lips press against hers. He feels a tinge of fear, a pang, amazement: how long can this last?

Slowly, they continue towards the shore, where they sit down in the shelter of a boat that has been drawn up on the beach.

They sit quite quietly, close to each other. A multitude of emotions swarm around inside him. Every movement he makes means a searing pain, a sudden glimpse of happiness, anxiety, a hushed calm.

She sits beside him and fills him with emotions, he interprets each of her smiles, tries to understand her eyes, chooses to touch her cheek, notes her slightest reaction.

There is no one else, they are completely alone. The only thing of significance is the line that appears over her eyes, the alertness awakened in him, the relief that ensues when she turns her eyes towards him.

For a long time they sit and are each other. They talk a little, they see and touch, they wait.

When he has taken her up to the house and has reached his cottage, he walks around.

He strikes one hand against the other. But it is the fast flow of feelings within him that really exists. His reflections as to what to do. The struggle between his hopes and his fear.

His path to a telephone is not a few steps, a drive and a few steps, but an irresistible urge, concern in case he seems too eager, a premonition of her laughter that will greet him in the telephone, a fear that she won't remember him, or hasn't time, a hope for an auspicious reply.

He rings her, and receives no message, no reply, but happiness, encouragement, a hope that is subsequently mixed with a little doubt.

He doesn't invite her out, but he chooses to create a new chance for a whole gamut of feelings, expectation, the joy of reunion, surprise at the changes that have taken place in her, the delight at touching her again, admiration, the fear of disappointing her, the satisfaction at awakening a smile, and the pain at having to part again, the fear, the fright, the want.

Only he doesn't ring again, he wonders and suffers for days on end, remembers and interprets every one of her movements.

They meet again a few times. They go for walks together,

they sit together in her car, they joke with each other, they try to understand each other, they talk to each other, they caress each other.

But actually, that is not what happens. For each of these single, visible movements, minute details in the great pattern, there is a vast number of feelings. It is not the movements that occur, it is the feelings that unfold, conflict with each other, strengthen each other, overcome each other.

He arranges to see her again. Irresolutely he walks backwards and forwards.

He takes his car to drive to his meeting with her. He is looking forward, he is wishing, he is reflecting.

She is already standing by the train, waiting for him. He feels a profound joy.

He runs across to her. He is totally absorbed by the beautiful sight, and the joy it awakens.

She tells him they can be together for the next three days. His head is filled with a multitude of possibilities.

STOLID

I drive up along the track faster than is justifiable, but I feel that nothing can stop me, no obstacles, no blow from the hand of fate that I can't avoid by dividing first. Twice I strike my head against the top of the car.

But I stop already at the first major crossroads. I don't know which road will offer me the quickest way to Diam. My first impulse is to choose one of the two roads at random, there can at most be a question of a quarter of an hour's difference in driving time. But a conviction that another segregation will choose the other possibility, thereby probably getting there first, makes me hesitate. I must have my map out and estimate the distance before I can choose.

Out on the main road I drive simply as fast as the car can go. I consider getting hold of a faster car, but at this time of the night it would probably be so difficult and time-wasting that I will get there sooner in my own.

Fresh plans keep coming to me all the time, new possibilities that have opened to me thanks to my discovery. So many ideas that I have difficulty in controlling my thoughts, ideas that I immediately have to reject, and others that spring out of me like segregations trying to realize themselves independently of me. It is a constant race.

I don't want others to go off with the good ideas, I keep trying my hardest to ensure the best ideas, the best designs, for myself; I have to force my way through a host of segregations of myself.

I have to increase my speed to be sure of getting there first. I drive at such a reckless pace that I have to place the car in the middle of the road, but there is no traffic, for it's night-time.

I don't know whether to take the time to convince Diam of the situation, or whether simply to hurry to make sure of her for myself, and then explain matters afterwards.

The car starts knocking, but I feel sure it will get me there. Another self tries to make me reduce speed, explaining that I will get there faster that way than by wrecking the car. That other self is out to slow me down. He is sitting beside me.

I try to push him out of the car; he grabs at the steering wheel. He hits me, he succeeds in jerking the wheel so that I have difficulty in straightening out; I manage it a little too late, and not quite enough; I'm out at the side of the road, on the verge; he's scared, too, and pulls at the wheel; we hit a tree.

I receive a blow on my head. It is not heavy, but it reduces the number of segregations, which is an advantage. Nevertheless, I remain stretched out on the ground. I stay there thinking the same thoughts so that a healthy segregation shall not rise from me and hurry on, I think the same thoughts. I can only limit them with difficulty.

I've managed for a long time, I don't know how long. I haven't thought; no more of me have emerged, they can't possibly.

They have tied me down. But quite gently so that I shan't discover it. They have taken me to a hospital. At last a car came along and stopped, I could only vaguely hear it because I had stopped thinking, so as to avoid it.

I have received a blow on the head. They think that's why I have to lie here.

I am all the time in some doubt as to whether to tell them everything, and explain about segregation so they can understand me, release me, praise me for the discovery. What a lot one can encompass within oneself.

But I know it will be difficult to convince them. I mentioned it to one of them, a doctor, he at least ought to be able to understand it. But he merely put on a show of kindliness. I don't know whether the other one, the one who grabbed at the steering wheel, is in this hospital as well. Perhaps he'll be telling them about it; if he does so before me he'll perhaps steal the credit, he'll receive all the honours. But as long as they keep me imprisoned here I can't do anything. Not unless there's someone I can rely on. It was a good job that doctor didn't believe me, he could start exploiting the discovery without more ado, before I get out.

I can't be quite sure that he's not already doing it. There's something wrong. I don't understand what.

Perhaps the discovery is too dangerous. But it was certainly necessary. It was necessary in order to save us, but now I'm having difficulty in taking care of it. It's as though it's trying to take control of me. I'm wasting away as a result of this constant segregation, that's the trouble. I hadn't realized that beforehand. But it's quite obvious. It must be stopped, I must get them to stop it.

I was able to before. I settle down quite quietly, I give up thinking so as to stop it. I must think the same thoughts, take care that no new ones come, the same one all the time. I can feel I'm succeeding. The same thought, I'm succeeding now, I only think that thought, the thought I'm allowed, the one that isn't dangerous. I can go on.

STOLIE

I don't understand what took hold of me.

Now, afterwards, it's a strange, empty feeling.

Of course it was a sensational insight that came my way. That might explain some of my actions, but it doesn't explain why I didn't think the matter through better.

That I could drive like a madman along the track, that I could try to get in ahead of myself. That I could actually have this feeling of seeing another segregation driving far ahead of me, only catching him up at the crossroads, where he was sitting studying a map.

That it could take me so long to realize that, despite these constant segregations, despite the fact that each of my two choices manifests itself in two versions of me, despite this *I* am not these other versions. Whatever they might experience will not be an experience for me. It will never be able to satisfy me that others have experiences in my place. On the contrary, it has a more or less depressing effect. I used previously only to know that there is a succession of possibilities that I shall never try, now I even know that there are others who do manage to try them, others who force themselves in and live in place of me. I feel a colossal envy towards these other I's to whom I'm related, but who found a better path than I, who had other experiences than I.

I returned calmly to the cottage, made sure that I gave myself as few possibilities for segregating as at all possible, so that there should be all the fewer to envy.

From now onwards, I must live as narrowly as I can, open up as few ways out as possible, limit every form of self-realization, shut myself in here.

By doing so I shall be least likely to feel any want for life.

The only way in which I can have all the experiences I dream about, enter into all the ramifications, is to make them up for myself.

My plan quite slowly takes shape. The novel must end up having a very special construction. It must begin with a meeting with Diam and then segregate into all the beautiful experiences I can ascribe to us. I can imagine how I shall soon have reached a hundred and twenty-eight delightful little episodes between us, one piquant, the second poetic, the third amusing, the fourth dramatic.

The only way of avoiding schizophrenia is to invent every single beautiful event I can conceive of, not one experience will I renounce, every one of them will have to be described with such total identification, with such understanding, that the experience will really become mine.

But then I realize that my meeting with Diam mustn't only lead to the beautiful experiences. I must also include the more problematical ones, those filled with conflict, for otherwise I will miss having gone through that kind of event with her.

But it will also be a limitation if I only make my meetings with Diam the subject of my fiction, for alongside them there is a whole range of experiences waiting for me. Consequently, I must start at an earlier stage. My novel must begin at the moment when I am deciding whether to meet Diam, or whether I would prefer the experiences that are independent of her. After this comes the first division.

The structure becomes clearer and clearer. I will have room to write about myself when sitting alone, missing Diam, an experience I would be sorry to do without. I will be able to invent long walks along the beach. These walks which so far have been a source of such delight to me, and which I must now renounce in the realistic world so as not thereby to create competitors for my experiences, but which on the other hand I shall be able to undertake in limitless numbers in the world of my imagination.

I can already now feel such a powerful urge to walk along the waterline, to hold Diam tight, that I can wait no longer. I must take out the first sheet of paper to make a start on my experiences.

STOREA

T he fact that our globular earth cannot properly be represented on a plain sheet of paper is something few will doubt. Before mapping it, it is necessary to decide on certain principles to be observed in the process. Following one principle will lead to a country being represented as rather elongated, following another will show it as being more dumpy. Neither of these two impressions is more 'correct' than the other.

This is a circumstance that has to be accepted concerning the physical – and in this sense quite simple – object that is our Earth.

It can hardly surprise anyone that the far more intangible, abstract and complex concept that we call an individual, is far more difficult to present on a flat sheet of paper, or in one long line such as is normally made up by the letters in a novel.

In order to portray the Earth more correctly, it would be necessary to use some object of roughly the same shape as the Earth itself: a globe. In order to depict an individual (or more correctly: the contents of an individual's mind over a short period of time) more precisely than the single-track novel form allows, it is necessary to find a structure more representative of 'the structure of the individual'. A characteristic feature of the human mind is the incessant expansion it is undergoing, the accumulation of incidents, feelings, experiences continually occurring, the constant encounter with new impulses and new ways. In short: to live is like placing oneself at the top of a pyramid and then trying to slide down all the sides at once. As everyone knows, there's a limit to how long that works.

So it seemed to me that the pyramidal structure I have used

in this book might possibly have some chance of providing a rather more accurate portrayal of an individual than has been possible in the single-track novel form.

But this led to the complication and the advantage that in portraying myself, I also found room for myself, that is to say the 'I' writing these lines.

This was an advantage because I really am able to include an important aspect of myself: that in which I appear as reader and interpreter of what I myself am writing, my role as what has been rather scornfully referred to as meta-narrator.

But at the same time it was a complication because I thereby introduce someone into my work who can quite easily become intolerable, that is to say the self-snooping, soul-searching, self-absolving raised finger.

I was once present at a performance by a conjuror who had such a love of the truth that he insisted on showing his audience how he did his tricks, at the same time as he was doing them.

At the moment I feel I'm in almost the same situation as that conjuror. In my respect for the truth, I have renounced trying to cheat my reader, whereby I precisely run the risk of cheating him, for he has no greater wish than to be cheated in an amusing manner.

But now I have set about it, I must try to utilize my space. I must continue in the role of the explicatory echo that threatens to prevent the actual words from being heard.

I conceive of this book as a fresh attempt on my part to take a further step in my effort to find the borderline which I am unable to cross.

I try constantly to live as abundantly as possible, to utilize my life as freely and richly as possible. And when this is done, and this book is finished, I can, by observing it, see which bonds have bound me, which rules I was unable to transgress, what notions I could not escape. And then I can start all over again. Try once more to break these bonds, rules, notions, so that, in my clumsy way, I can slide a little further down the pyramid.

STORES

Now, there is only one section of this book left for me to write: this one. Here at the end, I have interrupted the chronology because I have had an increasingly strong feeling that this section will give me difficulties and bring pain that I had hoped to be able to put off for some time. But I must tackle it.

I have looked through the book for a last time, and have convinced myself that it contains everything I can include in a comprehensive picture of myself, naturally still on the assumption that this present section, too, will be written and made true.

I think I have seldom written so slowly as is the case with these lines. Not because I have any great difficulty with the contents, for I know only too well what is to be written, nor because I am trying to present them in a particularly sophisticated style, for here a quite ordinary, leisurely, uncomplicated language will be sufficient.

When the section is finished, its last action completed, the manuscript of what is to become my masterpiece will be lying here on the writing desk in my cottage. I must hope that those who find it will understand how to treat it with the requisite respect.

For it is painfully obvious to me that this book can only achieve its purpose of providing a comprehensive account of me, my experiences, the whole range of moods to which life has subjected me, that it can only achieve this purpose and be complete if it also contains an honest description of my death.

So there is no way round this. There is no room for me once the work is finished.

One advantage I do gain from this: my life will be given as rounded and elegant a pattern as my book, in contrast to the unfinished lives that many people have to leave behind them.

It is relatively simple to construct a play confidently and elegantly, with a beginning that leads on to a climax and finishes with a snappy ending. It is far more difficult to fashion your life so that it steers a satisfactory course, for it is acted out on a temporary stage where you have to be prepared for the ropes holding up the curtain to snap at any moment, after which the curtain will irrevocably fall without any possibility of its ever being raised again, for which reason the play has to be abandoned. To construct a play so that every line in it could be used as the final effect is no mean task. You have even to be prepared for the possibility that the recalcitrant curtain will refuse to fall at the moment when you had originally hoped to end the performance, and then you have to be prepared to continue, without the audience suspecting problems, beyond the intended climax and snappy ending, and to improvise some means of extending the play without diminishing it.

My one advantage now, as I cut the rope guiding the drama of my life, is that I can myself ensure that the curtain falls immediately after the final point. However, this is an advantage I would happily renounce if by so doing I would not make my work false and ruin the novel – or, to use my own pedantic phrase, the short story collection – of my life. But I cannot go on living and thereby spoil the perfect structure of my work.

I have already made my preparations; all I need to do to complete them is to write these last lines.

There is a rowing boat on the shore. I have placed four heavy stones in it. As big as I could carry. In addition, there are four strong lengths of rope in the bottom.

I go down to the beach now. It is completely dark. There is a slight breeze, but that can't have any influence on my plan. I push the boat out on the water. I climb into it and begin to row.

I row a fair way out. When I am finally satisfied, I stop. I fasten a stone to each of my limbs. The problem is that I am a fairly strong swimmer, and I don't know what I might do when I become desperate in the water – perhaps my decision will suddenly no longer seem quite so obvious.

I put the four heavy stones on the gunwale, the boat heels over, but I keep as far away on the opposite side as the ropes permit.

I remember a charming little story, a Russian one, I think. I tell it to myself before I carry out my last act.

Somewhere in the world, the story goes, there is a wonderful little wand that can make everything disappear and change your life into a dream if you touch your head with it. If you don't like your life, then you just take this little wand and touch one of your temples with it – and suddenly, everything you didn't like will become a dream, and you will start on something quite new. Such is the little wand.

Before I change the entire contents of this book into a dream I wonder whether this is simply another spot where segregation will take place, after which my story will continue in two versions, one in hell and one in heaven.

I only need to go over to the other side of the boat and at the same time push one of the stones to make the whole thing overturn, dragging me down towards the water. Before hitting it I wonder whether I couldn't have continued my life under another name, or whether that, too, would have spoiled the book.

The water is colder than I reckoned with. I utter a loud scream that must be audible on the beach, but there is probably no one out there at this time of the night.

And then the stones carry out the task assigned to them in my story.

STORME

In the beginning, when there was only Adam, everything was simple. It was easy for Adam to be a human being, he had his own worth and his uniqueness as the basis of his life. Irrespective of what he undertook it would be right; it would form a myth and it would be remembered and told as the story of Adam. At any rate, it would establish him as a human being.

The situation now is quite different. There is a host of human beings, so many that only a quite small number of chosen ones can be fortunate enough to present themselves as individuals, to project themselves as anything but a grain of sand on a vast shore. And yet each one of this steadily growing number of human beings, every single one of them, has an irrepressible desire to authenticate himself as an individual, to present himself as the unique, original exemplar of humankind which he really constitutes. But no one is there ready to applaud his appearance; there are so many of us that we cannot conceivably see the special characteristics in every one of our fellow human beings. Most of us have to accept these conditions and drown or bury ourselves in the masses. And not even this action can be carried out in a genuinely tragical fashion. Every practicable way of destroying the self has long been presented on the world's arena.

We must face the fact that with the ever-increasing emphasis we place on society, and the ever-diminishing interest we can show in the individual, we cannot but develop in the direction of a state in which human beings can only be seen as the individual cells in a massive organism, a social body, in which the cells may well have different functions and be of

204

significance to each other, but in which the body cannot see its cells as being of any particular interest or individual value. In just the same way as we are unable to interest ourselves in the cells of which we are composed: if we scratch ourselves, we don't bewail the loss and mutilation of a number of cells, but bewail the reduced capacity of our body to function as it should.

The 63 I's portrayed in *Life at Night* live under such conditions. They are dependent on each other, prerequisites for each other, and they are all subject to the terrible fate of being on their way to the unknown. We feel how there are ever more of them, how they have to try to displace each other, how they each individually become more and more insignificant. Here we have a group of people each of whom feels the urge to be an Adam, a Shakespeare, an Einstein, but whose fate it is that there are two successors ready to take over their roles as soon as they have to renounce them. In that respect, they constitute a society.

It is impossible to read the book as though it were about only one person, as it itself maintains. It is impossible for anyone to have sexual intercourse so many times in three days, or to experience so many bouts of madness, so many smiles, so many catastrophes, so many vital decisions. When, nevertheless, the book so doggedly maintains that the 63 constitute one single person, it is precisely an attempt to enable the reader to understand the greater structure which these fleeting figures together constitute, the social being that the book presents.

But in this vast organism, the corpus represented by this book, there are naturally individual cells that distinguish themselves in some way, just as there are cells in our body which are of greater importance than others. Among the 63 sections the one you are now reading is distinguished by being the only one to note and describe this structure, and to accept its place as a minor element in the major framework. While the remainder are floundering in ignorance, preoccupied with their own little problems.

STORML

The rather special structure of this book might well confuse the unprepared reader, but once it is realized that this structure results in many more facets of the principal character, Alian Sandme, emerging than would be possible in a realistic form, it will be easier to become reconciled to it.

The technique employed by some painters dissatisfied with having to portray their models either *en face* or in profile, is well known. This was a technique enabling them to include both manifestations within the same face. A picture of this kind might at first sight appear to be alien or incomprehensible, but on closer consideration it can turn out to be particularly expressive.

This book employs a technique that can be considered the corresponding literary approach. So we should not become obsessed by the book's structure, but instead take an interest in its contents.

Alian Sandme must be seen as a normal individual, and the segregations he undergoes demonstrate the many possibilities, the enormous potential, possessed by the individual human being. On several occasions in the course of the book he himself refers to his sense of taking a further step, of making himself into himself, or rather: making himself still more in accordance with the person he is on his way to becoming.

(Note that the meta-formal structure is also repeated on a smaller scale, in the individual sentences. There are numerous examples of a special grammatical construction: the start of a sentence followed an element repeated, not synonymously, but in a slightly different sense. It is as though the sentence also runs into two or more possibilities, that it segregates, so to speak. The last sentence before this parenthesis might be seen as an example of this).

Let me illustrate this by means of a concrete example. In the section entitled SALME Alian and Diam have been talking together in the cottage. Diam becomes angry and leaves. Alian is left behind alone. Now there is no 'natural' continuation, no inevitable consequence of what has happened, such as a single-stranded story would have us believe. Alian *is* not a man to sit and twiddle his thumbs after such a confrontation, and Alian *is* not a man to run after the girl and seek to change her mind. He *is* not either of these two possible people. He can *turn himself into* one of the two, but in doing so he has changed, irrespective of which of the possibilities he chooses, he has gone beyond himself and found a new slough into which he can creep. Two roles, or places, are open to him. In fact, he doesn't fit either of them, but he turns himself into someone who does fit.

In any attempt to consider and understand the individual this book is about, it is necessary to look at two things: on the one hand what alternatives or what possibilities his imagination provides for him in the various situations in which a choice has to be made, and on the other in what way, how inventively, how well he realizes them.

In the book he is found in 31 situations where a choice has to be made (insofar as in the last 32 sections, those designated with 6 letters, no continuation is suggested; we don't know what segregations these will lead to). In a striking number the two possibilities can be described as, respectively, rational and romantic. Thus the first choice, S, indicates the romantic alternative (spending a couple of hours in order to make a ten-minute meeting with Diam) and the more earthbound alternative (of continuing the work on which he is engaged).

But the question is not even so simple. For the meeting with Diam can result in a consideration of their relationship (the rational), SAL, and in a more impulsive, active way out, SAN. And similarly, the book goes on in a reflective, deliberative vein, STO, and in a romantic corollary to the preceding reflections, STR.

So Alian must be seen as a man constantly torn between two elements within himself, two 'urges': the desire to launch himself into the incomprehensible world, to experience it, to renounce all rational argument; and on the other hand the need to understand, to investigate systematically, to reflect on the world, in order to discover a certain order in it. (Of course, denoting two precise opposites is a simplification, but the form of the book makes such a dualism almost obligatory). While this division into two is expressed theoretically, and therefore most precisely, in this section, its practical and therefore perhaps more entertaining formulation is to be found in the section entitled SANGER.

So Alian is torn between the impulsive and the reflective, the fairytale and the everyday, or the romantic and the rational. And who is not?

The next stage must be to examine in what way Alian realizes his potential. In so doing, we shall get closer to understanding Alian in his uniqueness, as an individual human being. An understanding of this kind I find to be a valuable experience for the reader.

If I were asked to name the people I know best, whose way of thinking I feel most familiar with, which I can empathize with, perhaps a dozen or so of the ones I mentioned would come from my closest circle of acquaintances and family, a couple I would have come across in films or on the stage, while perhaps fifty or so would be characters from novels.

That tells us something about where we find a large

proportion of our knowledge of the world. And it also tells us something about why it will be valuable to try to achieve a fuller understanding of Alian, a person whom we have already met in an unusual range of widely differing situations.

Such an examination can be arranged in two ways. You can leap into it, take an interest in the feelings that Alian's behaviour has awakened in you, or you can go about it in a more carefully considered manner.

STREGE

I go home to the cottage. I don't walk particularly quickly, though I am not tired.

When I get inside I don't settle down to write, and I don't settle down to read. But this isn't because I feel ill or out of sorts.

I sit there staring into the air, where, actually, there is nothing particular to see.

An hour later, I am already thinking of going for a walk again, but I find the idea quite ridiculous. I don't need more exercise or fresh air. I persuade myself to stay where I am.

The following morning I get up earlier than usual. I dress hurriedly and go out before I've had any breakfast. I walk across to the house I visited the previous evening.

There are two young men there, tidying up. One of them is wearing braces and is crawling around on the floor to sweep it with a broken-handled broom. I hesitate for a moment, but just as the other one is about to say: 'What do you want here?' I hurry to say: 'I just wanted to thank you for a nice evening yesterday.'

'Oh, you were there, too?' he asks. He has a fat cigar stump between his lips, turning it round without the help of his fingers.

'Yes. Incidentally, I met a girl. She forgot something ... a ball pen ... she forgot it in my pocket.'

'Where did she forget it?'

'Yes, I promised to hold it for her and I put it in my pocket without thinking, and then I forgot to give it back to her. It looks rather expensive, I think it's gold.'

'Gold? Was there a girl here with a gold ball pen – good

Lord! May I see it?'

'I haven't got it here. I left it at home, locked in a safe deposit box, I didn't dare carry it around with me.'

'No, obviously.'

'Do you know where I can find her? She's called Kerianne.'

'Kerianne? There's no one by that bloody name as comes here. Do you know anyone called Kerianne?'

The man with the braces looks up and wipes his nose.

'Nah. But I found a piece of paper a bit ago. There was something like that on it. It's probably in the rubbish bin over there.'

There is a crumpled piece of paper lying amongst dust and ashes and matches. I take it and smooth it out. The name Kerianne is written on it, and then a telephone number.

'That must be a message she's left for me,' I exclaim. 'She must have discovered the ball pen had gone, so she left a message for me. May I copy it?'

'You can have it. And you haven't got a ball pen to write with, either. You'd better go home to your safe deposit box.'

They are laughing as I leave, but I take no notice. As soon as I arrive home, I get into the car and drive to town to ring. I know where the nearest telephone booth is and make straight for it. But there is an excited young chap in working clothes in it. He is waving his arms about and gesticulating so much that he must lose at least a kilo as a result of this conversation.

When I finally get to the phone I can't find the note. I know which pocket I put it in, but it isn't there. But of course, I can remember the number. I haven't tried to memorize it, but I've looked at the paper a couple of times to admire her name, and so the number has stuck with me.

When I manage to dial the number, I am very surprised that it is some office lady answering even before I have started to listen.

'Could I speak to Kerianne, please?' I say, in some confusion.

'Kerianne, who? We've no Kerianne her. I think you must have the wrong number. We haven't any Kerianne here, have we?'

This last question is not directed at me, but to someone at the other end of the line.

'Just a moment. She's coming.'

The lady has changed her tune so quickly that once more I have to pull myself together.

'Hello, it's me.'

'Is that Kerianne?' I say, although I can be in no doubt after hearing the voice.

'Yes, it's Kerianne.'

'It's Alian. It was me ... I was one of those you went for a walk with on the beach yesterday. It's me with the ball pen.'

'Hello, Alian. It was nice of you to ring.'

'Do you think so? I'm not disturbing you, am I?'

'No, not really.'

'I promise to be quick. I wanted to ask you whether you don't think we could meet some time, one evening, just to have a chat. I didn't manage to say much.'

'That's not a particularly good idea, Alian,' she says in a sad voice. 'You see, I'm married.'

'That's all right. So am I.'

She laughs.

'I can't very well make it in the evenings. You see I'm usually together with my husband.'

'What about yesterday?'

'What do you mean? Oh, I was together with him then, too. He was just so busy with other things that he didn't notice I went for a short walk. But perhaps we could have lunch together in my lunch break?'

213

'Yes, that would be lovely. Today. When?'

'I have my lunch break at one o'clock. We can meet then.'

She rings off while I'm still standing bowing and saying thank you and I'm looking forward to it. It is only afterwards I realize that I don't know her address. But the telephone book sees to that.

It is so late that it isn't worth driving back to the cottage. Instead, I drive a short way along the main road. And after turning round so as to be back in good time to pick her up, I run out of petrol right out there on the main road. I have a reserve can in the boot, but it's empty. I size up the situation and decide that it can't be more than a couple of kilometres to the nearest petrol station, and I set off running with the empty can in my hand.

There's a limit to how long I can carry on running fast if I am to have any hope of finishing the course. I continue at a slower pace, look at my watch every other minute, and work out how much late I'm going to be.

I get the can filled. I run back, even more slowly than before. I try taking long, winning strides and then quick, light steps, but both of them make me breathless from the exertion.

I reach the car at ten past one. I am in such a rush that I empty half the petrol down the outside. I start the car and discover that I'm sitting with the cover from the petrol tank in my hand. I run round and screw it on. And at last drive off in the direction of the town.

It's twenty past when I arrive. To my surprise she is waiting for me.

I jump out and start explaining.

'It'll be a quick lunch,' is all she says, before I have told her about my mishap.

Sitting in a restaurant, we suddenly have nothing to say to each other.

So I say, 'I almost couldn't find you. They didn't know anyone called Kerianne at the house.'

'Neither do I,' she says with a laugh.

I like her laughter. I am still afraid she only wants to meet me because she thought I had something important to say.

'What are you called, then?'

'I'll tell you that next time.'

'Next time?' I blurt out in my amazement.

'Yes, I suppose you intend to give me a proper meal some time and not fob me off with a snack like today?'

'All right, if you'll tell me your name in exchange.'

She takes hold of the pendant I have hanging round my neck, and lifts it off. It is a heart, with Mea's name engraved on one side.

'I'll have it engraved on this,' she says. 'That is, if you don't mind.'

'That's just the right place for it. But you'd better make do with your initial, just in case.'

I have a feeling that my life is moving towards a fresh series of stories. She looks at me confidently and attentively; I return her glance expectantly and warmly, as when in anticipation you let your eyes embark on the first sentence in a book you have long been looking forward to reading.

STREGL

I go down to the beach. I stand looking out across the water. Go back to the place where I gave her the ball pen. I can see the tracks we have made in the sand at this spot.

Then I walk decisively up towards the house. And stop decisively and turn round and go down to the shore. Stand and look out across the water. Walk to and fro a little. Then I pull myself together and make for the house. Stop for a moment before reaching it. Go a little further away from the house again.

I stand down on the beach, realize that I can't achieve anything in this way. Indecisively, I drift up towards the house, and try the door. It is locked. I have to go round and find another door. Only a few guests remain. Four or five young people are hanging around, unable even to pull themselves together for a bout of drinking or sexual excesses.

'Hello, has Kerianne gone?'

'No, she's never been here.'

'I was with a girl from here, earlier this evening. There's a message I forgot to give her. I wanted to get hold of her again.'

They simply give me a lethargic look and reply by shaking their heads, or nodding when there's something they've understood. I describe Kerianne, in phrases as subdued as possible so as not to shock them. No one nods in recognition. I ask whether she usually comes here. There is no reaction.

I have to go again without achieving anything. There is something about the task that appeals to me.

I note such information as I have: Her first name, which might well be false, but is very pretty. If it's an assumed name, then at least I know a name she might well assume, which tells

216

me about her imagination. A house which she has visited, apparently without any, or at least many, of the guests knowing her. She might have been invited just as much by chance as I was. That shows that she might have the habit of taking a walk along the shore, unless she was picked up somewhere or other, for instance by a car-load on its way to the party stopping to ask her the way. On the other hand, this possibility encompasses other information. In addition, I have the marks she has made in the sand. For a moment I consider taking a plaster cast of her footmarks, but realize that it will scarcely be of any use in my search.

It is obvious to me that it will be an enormously demanding task. But it is a task with perspectives, with a great wing span: a lifetime spent in searching for the woman I loved!

I hurry home to the cottage so as not to waste any time. Now the search must be organized rationally and systematically. I have to accept that in fact I can scarcely remember what she looked like, hazy as I was as a result of the situation, or perhaps of what was in the glass. All the more beautiful, freer will it be to search for her: I am not even sure that I would recognize her if I met her by chance. But also it would feel a little unfair if without any effort on my part I came across her through a chance meeting.

I fill two sheets of paper with the information I have and the possibilities I am able to discern at the moment. The following morning my optimism has diminished considerably. I walk about haphazardly in the neighbourhood without making any progress. It is obvious that my task is becoming more difficult with every passing day, because the memories become fainter.

I have known the experience it is to seek experience, but when it starts to seem hopeless the pleasure is lessened.

I sit there flicking aimlessly through my notes. I feel angry that my life is arranged so badly. It seems aesthetically unsatisfactory to me if I am to have my life ruined simply because on one single occasion, in a confused situation, I forgot to ask for a telephone number. It can't be arranged that badly.

I can see only one way out if I am to make good the damage: I must turn back the clock.

I find the note I wrote just before my meeting with Kerianne. I concentrate on what I have written. And because it so accurately recapitulates what I thought, I manage completely to recapture the mood I was in at that time.

I name the person who is the cause of the old note, and of the note I have just read through, calling this person me. This implies that time has elapsed.

My heart is pounding against the edge of the table as I get up to consider the new situation.

First I convince myself that there isn't too much life in the fireplace. I leave some of the lights on so as to be able to find my way back more easily, lock the cottage and walk out into the night.

Now I know where I am. I increase my speed, rush through the next episode as when you run a film too quickly, or quickly flick through a manuscript.

I hurry down to the shore. See a man on a pole. Jump up on another. His lips are moving enormously quickly. He jumps down, I jump down. We hurry off, in different directions. I approach a house where there is a man coming towards me.

For a moment I am on the point of turning off down to the beach, but I manage to alter my decision.

Like seeing a film run at many different speeds, only stopping, reducing speed when you change the spool, to make sure that you choose the right continuation.

I walk with him up to the house. There are countless

people getting up, rushing to and fro, coming and going. I look across at the girl opposite me, who looks at me as though she knows me.

Outside, I think of all the stories one has come across about people who were allowed to live part of their lives over again, and who inevitably landed back in the same groove, a necessary consequence of the view that men live in a straight line: if you start at one end, you must inevitably arrive at the other. I am pleased I don't share this view, that I believe people can decide for themselves which way to go. Accordingly, I fix the question of Kerianne's telephone number in my mind so as to be quite sure of remembering to ask it when, before long, we are walking down on the beach, so that I can lead us in a better direction.

I am almost too late. She gets up and gives me an angry look. I reduce my speed to normal. The things I expect to happen, do happen. I become absorbed in the action, leap into my role.

I calmly get up and walk across to the garden door.

The girl who was sitting opposite me is standing in the middle of the doorway. She sees me, smiles and makes to step aside. Something or other lifts my hand and makes it stroke her surprisingly soft hair.

'Keep your fingers to yourself,' she says, making to smack my hand, which is already gone.

'Take it easy. There was a bit of fluff.'

I hold out a piece of fluff and flick it away before she sees there was nothing there.

'I'm sorry if my attentions were unwelcome,' I say. 'But have you had that dress for long?'

She looks at me, uncomprehending.

'I'll explain. I'm a dress designer. This very day, I've designed the dress to end all dresses. So much of it is routine

219

work, you know, but today I wanted to make something absolutely original and personal, something for the very special woman. You'll understand that I was surprised when I saw you dressed in the model I designed this afternoon.'

STRENG

The encounter with her breasts is so breathtaking that I forget to continue my story when my hand reaches them. They are soft and particularly receptive to my hand's caresses. I have a feeling that they move towards my hand, reach out for it as I move it away.

I have plenty of time to think about the unusual aspect of this situation in which I am lying in a strange house together with a strange girl whom I have seduced by means of a long series of ever more stimulating stories.

One of my hands is busily occupied with giving her breasts artificial respiration, as soon as it releases one of them that one begins to lose its breath and cry out for more massage. My free hand is moving in under the lower hem of her dress. In the darkness it is slowly making its way up towards her panties, and in under them.

Meanwhile, Parliette's hands are cautiously opening my trousers and extracting what they can find there. Thereby it is revealed that my words have contained bigger promises than my trousers. While my hands continue their judicious task, hers are kindly reciprocating, but to no avail.

She is becoming ever more lively beneath my caresses. By means of a joint effort we make easier my access to her breasts; unaided, I remove her panties. She slides over on to her back, with her mouth open, my fingers move around as quickly as did my tongue a moment ago. Far too quickly she reaches the climax and the snappy ending.

We lie quiet for a time. Then she is given leave to experience another little adventure, with a sophisticated ending that lasts far longer than usual.

After yet another pause we terminate the coupling with a glorious bang, a brief surprise ending.

Try as she might, we never succeed in getting my built-in ball pen in the mood for telling stories. In the end, we have to give up, she gently pats the soft thing that continues to hang its head, after which she puts it back in its place.

'You couldn't talk your way out of that,' she says, smiling sweetly.

I am immediately on the defensive; on the one hand I have an energetic propaganda speech prepared to the effect that through its worship of male potency society is creating the impression that men ought to be able at any time and in any place, and with anyone or anything, and for this very reason it instils in men a fear of not being able, thus resulting in difficulties. On the other hand I have a romantic explanation to the effect that she is so much a woman, and that I am so obsessed with the cult of womanhood that I couldn't bear the responsibility of touching her.

But I manage, in time, to keep both explanations to myself, realizing that they would not put me in a better light.

'No, it was probably a good thing our meeting was cancelled,' I say instead. 'I don't think my story could have won.'

She is still smiling a little; I daren't make a judgement as to whether it is my own incapacity that is the cause of the smile.

'Shall we be seeing each other again?' I say carelessly.

I still have some days before I expect to be leaving the cottage.

'If you like I could fetch you one day so you can see my cottage.'

She seems sceptical.

'You might like to see my collection of stories, it's quite a size.'

She agrees. We arrange an evening and a place where I can find her.

'But you mustn't expect anything,' she says in a decisive tone. 'I'm not interested in stories that are written down. And incidentally, I had no intention of going to bed with you. But I can't resist having stories told to me.'

As I leave, I have already begun to arrange a new sequence of stories intended not only for a female audience, but arranged in such a way that they can also have an uplifting effect when heard by male ears.

STRENO

When my hands reach her breasts I become so preoccupied that I forget to go on telling stories. The girl immediately gives a start, and she tries to pull herself away from me.

'I'm sorry,' I say. 'I forgot myself. I just happened to think of a dream I had the other night, and so I forgot where I was.'

'What was that dream about?'

'It was pretty strange, very detailed and yet curiously vague as dreams tend to be. I met a pretty girl who seemed to be fairly experienced and attractive. But for some reason or other it was immediately clear to me in the dream that she knew nothing at all about the other sex, had grown up without having heard of or seen any man. So now it became my task to teach her the most elementary things. I got her on to a bed beside me and pressed myself against her. And she found that quite natural, while she examined my face with great interest with her fingers. Then I pulled up her dress a little, like this, well, even higher, until her beautiful breasts were laid bare. Then I placed my mouth against one of them. I pushed as much of it into my mouth as I could, like that, and could feel the tip of it against my palate.'

It's difficult for me to talk with so much in my mouth, but I daren't stop for a moment for fear she might regret it again.

'Now I took the girl's hands, both of them, while kissing her, like this, gently, and then more passionately; she learned amazingly quickly, while I took her hands and guided them down to my trousers, and with their help I got them open, like this, and persuaded them to take a warm and gentle hold around the stiff stick that to her amazement and my own satisfaction I kept down there. She quickly learned to let her hand drift up and down it, while my hands drifted across her breasts and brought them more and more to life, to her amazement and my satisfaction. Occasionally, her hands forgot to attend to the task they had been set to, but then they only needed a little encouragement to get going again. I let my hand drift slowly and gently down over her panties. I could feel the hair beneath and could sense that she was understanding more and more of what I was teaching her.'

I have so many irons in the fire, keeping her hands moving, my hands moving, and not least my tongue moving, so that only for a brief instant do I have time to think of what I am doing. I am silent for a moment, the movement of her hands ceases, and my member begins to lose its intensity. I hurry to continue, and am soon on course again.

'I let my hand drift in under her panties, she was warm and soft and wet, but also uncomprehending. I touched her gently, like that and like that, and erased her surprise with kisses that she understood better and better. Gently, I teased her panties down, although I could hardly spare a hand to do it. Her calm, exploring movements on my member had made me quite ready, and I could feel that she, too, was ready to experience the greatest surprise. I drew her close to me, got her to move her hands, like that, and pressed myself gently up into her, like that. I left my hand on her crotch, I moved quickly, played about with my fingers on her breast and in her crotch, and kissed her, all at the same time, like that and like that, I could feel she was coming, I increased my own tempo. She came and gave out a long, gratifying cry, all on her own initiative, while I hurried to increase my speed still more and finished my task.'

I have to stop talking, as I come. Parliette seems to accept this, she makes no sign of wanting to draw back.

We stay in each other's arms. My vocal chords feel quite

rough now. I make to help her again, but she stops me. I try to pull myself together to tell her a little more, but this, too, she stops, to my relief. We lie there.

'Thank you,' she says in a fairly friendly tone. I murmur a similar expression of gratitude.

She begins to gather her clothes around her.

'I tend to find it difficult to get any pleasure from it because I easily come to wonder whether I *can* get any pleasure from it, and that's enough to make it impossible for me.'

'Yes, indeed, I know that one, too,' I say with unaccustomed frankness.

'But as a matter of fact, I was so absorbed by what you were telling me that I forgot to create any problems for myself.'

'I'm delighted. When can we see each other again? I know some more stories.'

'It's no use. Next time I'll start thinking that you're telling me stories to make me forget that perhaps I can't. And then I can't.'

I consider this problem.

'I must be able to find another method next time,' I promise optimistically.

'And I'll immediately think: Now he's using a different method to stop me wondering ... and so on. It won't work.'

While I'm looking for a way out she has dressed.

'I hope I shan't see you again,' she says. 'But thanks for the story.'

She goes in to the others and shuts the door in a rather determined fashion behind her. I slip out with an empty feeling all over. It feels as though I've been to bed with a handful of warm words.

At the same time I am amused to think that, for the first time, I have been able to use my products as the basis for an exchange of goods. So stories are of some use after all, I conclude, and give my silent member an encouraging thought.

But at the back of my mind there is still an empty feeling as when you have been through a short story that fails to make its point.

STRIDE

I rrespective of what I do, he unconcernedly continues his walk. I run around him, wave my hands in front of his eyes but without making him blink. He seems to be pondering some problem, I have a clear feeling that I know which. He is walking right down by the water's edge in the firm sand. I shout in his ear, whistle, blow at him, it makes no difference. On the contrary it seems to me that I have less and less effect. I pick up some stones and fling them at him. They strike him so gently that he thinks it's the breeze he can feel.

He reaches some posts on which a man is sitting. He passes the time of day with him and sits down. They discuss some arcane problem, about how they never have any new experiences, while all the time I'm jumping up and down in front of them. The other chap can't see me either. I try with all my might to tip him off the post, while he says that after reproduction nothing new happens to humankind, there is no prospect of new experiences, until the dissolution of identity takes place.

Can what I am experiencing at this moment be a sample of the dissolution of identity? At all events, the man is sitting there completely immovable, until he himself decides to hop down.

The man who is exactly like me, who has now taken my place, begins to walk back. He approaches a house, where a man carrying a bottle comes towards him.

Then something happens that confuses me still more than the incident when I found the man at home in the cottage. The man divides, suddenly there are two of them. Apparently without having any sense of each other's existence the two editions continue each in his own direction, one going up towards the house, the other away from it. I hesitate, have no idea which of them I ought to follow, to whom I belong. My first impulse is to follow the man going up to the house, but I realize that it will be still more difficult to make contact with him when he is surrounded by so many people.

While I am considering this I have a feeling that yet another version comes rushing along at the double, meets yet another man carrying a bottle, and continues his way up towards the house without reducing his speed.

I follow the man who is walking along the shore pursued by two drunken men. First, I turn round to see whether another shadow is segregating from me and making for the house, but I see no one.

The man jumps over a hedge. Only with difficulty can I follow him as I am out of breath after all the confusion.

Nothing can surprise me any longer, so when he again divides, like a sleepwalker I follow the man who is heading back to the cottage, hoping to slip in through the door at the same time as he, in, so that I have the chance of a rest.

There is light in the windows, but no one is sitting in the chair, as I feared for a moment, although it would amuse me to see this man standing outside the window and knocking in vain.

The man unlocks the door and goes in without my having the slightest opportunity to slip in with him. He locks the door behind him and settles down triumphantly, comfortably, contentedly.

I hang around the cottage for some time yet, but without achieving any result. At last I give up. I leave the cottage and start roaming around.

After wandering about for a long time I find a shed, in which I sleep for a couple of hours, covered by some damp sacking. I go this way and that way, aimlessly, without any plans. Irrespective of where I meet people none of them notice me.

I live on fruits and berries, and whatever I see an opportunity to pinch. However, this is no great problem to me, as I can go wherever I want, unseen. It surprises me that, despite my poor physique, without being able to attract any interest, I can still feel hungry, cold and weary.

I clamber up on the back of a lorry and am carried a couple of hours' drive from my point of departure. Then I continue to drift around, unable to find a place anywhere, unable to establish myself an identity in people's minds.

Late one night, when I have been unable to find a suitable place to sleep, I am walking, tired and dispirited, through a forest. I notice some lights and soon find myself approaching a house from which smoke is rising. I get as far as the window. In the sitting room I can see a man sitting at a writing desk. He is busy, apparently with a balance sheet or something of the sort. Once more I vainly try to gain some interest by knocking on the window.

I prowl about near the house for a time, until I notice that one of the doors is not closed, but is standing ajar. With great difficulty, I manage to force my way through the crack, and find myself standing inside, in the warm room. Naturally, the man has not noticed anything. He goes on with his work.

There is a bookcase behind him. On the top shelf there is a metal bust representing some author or other. I tiptoe across behind him. With an enormous effort I overturn a row of books so that, as they fall, they knock over the bust, which is already tottering on the narrow bookshelf, whereby it overbalances and with a heavy blow lands on the top of the man's head. He collapses; I can be in no doubt that he is dead.

He has just about fallen out of his chair. Wearily, I seat

230

myself in it and take a look at what he was working on. A pile of papers covered with writing is lying there. I read the last lines he has written.

'I prowl about near the house for a time,' it says. 'Until I notice that one of the doors is not closed, but is standing ajar. With great difficulty, I manage to force my way through the crack, and find myself standing inside, in the warm room. Naturally, the man has not noticed anything. He goes on with his work.'

I feel giddy and exhausted. I must have lost consciousness for a moment. The man I have killed must be my author. I have only been a character in his book. No wonder I have been so powerless, so shadowy.

I feel, not as though I have dreamt the whole of this affair, but as though I have only been written into it. Slowly I seem to regain a little strength. I look at the last sentence on the paper: 'And with a heavy blow lands on the top of the man's head,' it says.

I take the ball pen that has fallen out of the man's hand, intent on taking over his place, his position, making myself the author of my own story.

STRIDT

I take a long run and rush at him with all my might. When I strike him he has reached exactly the spot where I originally felt that surprising jolt. I fall over, have hurt myself a little; his hand, which up to now has been in his pocket, is pulled out by the collision, and with it the key that falls down in the sand.

He looks round in amazement, doesn't notice me lying there on the ground groaning. He continues his walk, without noticing the loss of the key.

When he has gone and I have had time to think, I pick up my key again. I immediately feel considerably more confident and self-assured, knowing I am in possession of it.

I go home to the cottage where there is still a light in the windows. I let myself in and feel at ease again.

I am not far from convincing myself that the experience with the double has been a dream or the result of a rather excessive imagination. I look around, nothing has been changed in the cottage, no trace to indicate that there have been others here apart from myself.

I read a little. Stand at the window and look dreamily down towards the sea, naturally I occasionally have the impression that I can see a figure on its way up towards me, but just as naturally it turns out each time to have been an optical illusion.

This vision I have had gives me food for thought. I sit down to write a note on it, as the experience will probably find a place in my next novel.

I let my eyes skim over the top sheet of paper. It contains an account about which I know nothing, which I don't remember and which I don't recall having written. And yet there is no doubt that it is written in my hand.

I search in a state of some excitement, find the beginning of the story and settle to read it:

'The event is now so distant, or the situation seems so stable, that I dare to mention it. I will hurry to do so before it fades from my memory. Even now it is strangely distant and unreal.

Ten days or so ago, I had an amazingly beautiful dream. Everything in it was as easy and natural as it can only be in dreams and memories.

In the dream I met a girl who was suddenly standing before me enveloped in her natural, calm beauty. She was not pushing and not reticent; completely at ease we were able to go for a walk together through the wood. When we parted she uttered some words that even in the dream made me uneasy: that we should meet again the following night.

At that moment I awoke to my customary void. I began to walk around, walked for most of this day, I felt I had a fever coming on, continued to walk about until I was so tired that I collapsed on to my bed.

Again I found myself in this dream in which everything seemed natural and significant. I'm walking arm in arm with the girl in an ethereal environment, talking to her, joking with her. Together we stand by the sea and watch the sun rise.

My next day was just as idle and futile as the previous one. I did what I could to get through it quickly, remember nothing of what I undertook, until finally I could sleep again.

Now I felt at quite home in the land in which the dream took place. The girl introduced me to other people whom I found lively and interesting. We enjoyed ourselves together, no one found me a stranger, I seemed to slip naturally into the surroundings.

I had to drag myself through the next day, too, as through a long drawn-out dream that can't bring itself to finish.

The dream now occurs just as surely as my everyday life does when I waken up. It even seems to me that people have been waiting for me in the dream. I move freely in and out of this new place. I run together with the girl, we try to catch each other while running in the sand.

Consequently, I am quite tired when the day comes, so I almost sleep my way through it.

Until night finally comes; then I liven up and go in to my friends.

My stay with them is only disturbed by the arrival of day, I must lie down and rest in order to sleep the dull day away.

Soon I am altogether able to change my place of abode, so that my waking, living, real life is spent in these surroundings and with these people whom a few days ago I only knew from my dream, while the time I spend in what I previously called my world is now blurred, meaningless and alienated from real life for me.'

I sit there for some time after reading to the end.

It seems clear to me that this account has been written by the man I met in the house, the man who entirely resembled me and who, then, not only writes with my handwriting, but also expresses himself in the same way as I. If his account is anything but a free fantasy on his part I must assume that he has succeeded in transferring to his 'dream realm'. The similarity between us leads immediately to the theory that the man I surprised in here is simply myself as I live in my dream world. Our surprising meeting is due to the fact that for some reason or other I found myself for a time in both the realistic world and the fantasy world. Normally, we avoid meeting because when one is asleep the other is awake.

I feel tired after all these experiences, need to sleep, but am not keen to do so as long as I am so obsessed by these fantasies.

One more thing is unclear to me: Has my double written down the account for his own use, or because he wanted to communicate with me, to introduce me to the life that I secretly live in my dreams?

STRIME

Askaron has turned off along a forest path. I turn the same way and hurry to catch him up. Apparently without having seen me he increases his speed at the same time so that the distance between us remains the same.

I know this area well, and hope I can catch him up by using a short cut that we shall soon be reaching. But he, too, knows the short cut and makes use of it.

I stop to consider the situation, he does the same. He is so close that I could reasonably hope to attract his attention by shouting, but actually I have nothing concrete to talk to him about, and I don't know him particularly well, so I feel it would seem pushing to speak to him in that way.

He sets off again, and I follow passively. Suddenly I pull myself together, ignore all conventions, make my way forward and have almost caught up with him when he is about to increase his speed. I am so close to him that I can address him without appearing pushing. He stops.

'I'm glad I met you,' I admit. 'It's not often you meet people at this time.'

'Yes, I've got into the habit of staying up late, so that I have the quiet of the night to myself.'

'Yes, I do the same thing.'

I observe him keenly, to see what characteristics he has adopted that can enrich me. But there does not appear to be anything visible, perhaps it's a question of a new insight he has acquired.

'I was just thinking of you,' I say. 'We've never exchanged more than a few remarks. And yet I have a feeling of knowing you quite well. Even if you can still do things that surprise

236

me.'

'Yes, I well understand what you mean. And now you're going to say that you often observe me to see what message I have for you.'

'Yes, I've often had the feeling that now I was as I wanted to be, and then, when I've met you I have recognized some quality with which I have wanted to enrich myself.'

'Yes, I've noticed that. I'm glad you've progressed so far that you feel you want to talk to me about it. Whatever you do, you mustn't think your copying me has bothered me. On the contrary, I have felt flattered that someone who is pretty reasonable and pleasant has been able to use me, has felt I could teach him something. And furthermore it has often been a kind of spur to me as it were to have you at my heels, a challenge to my imagination, my ability to renew myself. But I feel that now you have progressed so far that I ought to tell you the truth. I really don't exist. No, don't laugh. Of course I exist as a physical person, and you can see me, hear me and touch me. But the man you imagine, the man you are trying to live up to doesn't exist, he is only a projection of your own imagination, your own aims and ambitions, which you are assigning to me. Perhaps you were a little more satisfied with the developmental stage that you yourself had reached than you felt you should be. And therefore you invented a motive force that could effect a further impetus to the development of your personality. And by chance you used me for that purpose.'

'Is that the message you can give me today?'

'Yes, the message that you have no need of an external model, that you only need to search deep inside yourself in order to sense the man you would now like to become.'

For once, I feel the meeting with Askaron to be a disappointment. His words seem stilted, psychologizing and laboured. I have a feeling he is hiding something from me. I happen to notice a medallion he is wearing, that reminds me of my own. At that moment not only do I feel my heart medallion strike against my chest, but also a movement within my chest.

'Thanks for the chat,' I say. 'I was glad I could manage to talk to you. I've got something to think about now.'

He stays behind, standing as proudly as if his son had been nominated Pope. As soon as I am out of sight I increase my speed. I quickly return to the cottage. And get into the car.

I drive up towards Dahle. It has started to get light. I drive calmly and with restraint. I am deliberating, laying a plan of action.

I make straight for the telephone booth. Diam has gone south alone. I don't know her hotel, but I know which town she is in.

It is more difficult than I think. But after ringing around for an hour or so, I finally find an hotel that will admit to having a guest called Diam. I ask to be put through to her room.

It *is* Diam who at last answers the phone. She sounds heavy with sleep.

'Hello, Diam. It's Alian. Can you hear me? I'm sorry if I woke you.'

'Hello, Alian. What gave you the idea of ringing to me?'

'That's too long a story to tell here. I just needed to hear your voice. I didn't get time to come to the train, you see I was snowed under with work, and it was such a short stop in any case.'

'But I didn't really expect you to come, either. There's no need to apologize.'

'Can you find a little time for me if I come and visit you?'

'Well, but where are you? Aren't you in Dahle now?'

'Yes, but I can soon get there.'

'That would be lovely. To be honest, I've met a friend, Doria. And she can take my place and give me an alibi. So we can be all on our own for the next couple of days if you can come. That would be lovely.'

'I'm on my way.'

As I start the car I think that I can probably find a better guide for my life than this Askaron, and hang my medallion up on the driving mirror.

STRIML

B ut the man in front of me seems to be far from giving up the ghost, on the contrary, he is moving off at a speed that only just allows me to follow him without losing even more ground.

The chase lasts for over half an hour, during which time I don't gain on him. During this process I have ample opportunity to admire the rather irregular gait he employs, as though one leg is a shade longer than the other, and which I acquired long ago. This was all the easier to do as my right leg really is a little shorter than the other. I could easily hide this defect, but have found it opportune to let it appear in my manner of walking, so that even the sound of my footsteps expresses my own special personality. I once told a girl that the irregularity arose when I was exchanging legs with another man, who went and regretted it when the bargain was half fulfilled. However, the girl showed no sign of believing my explanation, for which reason I have not produced it since.

By putting his best leg forward in this way Askaron reaches Dahle, which has obviously been his objective. Before I know where I am, he has disappeared. I hurry over to the place where I last saw him, but just then become aware of a house I haven't noticed before.

Now, I don't usually keep a record of the number of houses on my way, just as I only rarely count the trees I pass, but nevertheless, it seems to me that the building which I am facing has to an unusual degree been able to hide from my erratic glances. The house is not lit up, except that a narrow beam of light is escaping from the door. I look around, to convince myself that this must be the place that has swallowed

Askaron. When my eyes once more wish to rest on the house, it appears to them that it is no longer there. When, in some confusion, I have looked around me again, I feel reassured to discover that my eyes will now again acknowledge this object.

I don't normally force my way into houses where I have no errand, but in this case I make an exception, intent as I am on achieving a conversation with Askaron. I enter with a carefree remark on my lips: 'I'm sorry, the house wasn't here when I walked into it.' But I have no need of it.

I am standing in a dark room, only lit up by the small amount of light that is not seeping out through the narrow crack by the door. I can't find any door that will take me further, it is as though the house ends just as abruptly as it has appeared, but only too suddenly do I discover another way forward as I fall down an unlit and unprotected staircase.

There is no more light in the cellar, where I lie pulling myself together, but I can hear sounds as though from a party. While my back is growing accustomed to this new way of using a staircase, my eyes begin to wander around in the dark. When I am able to stand again I can see four or five doors for me to choose between.

I enter a room that is quite well lit, not least considering that I have been fumbling around in the dark for so long. There is a motley company assembled there, no one seems to take any notice of my entrance.

I can see Toran Lynde sitting in an alcove with a tankard. He is alone, thin-lipped and expressionless. When he notices me he gives me an angry look, as though it is I who have introduced him to a company in which he doesn't feel at home.

I hurry on, pretending to be unconcerned. In the next alcove there is a loud-voiced and emancipated assembly. Although I don't recognize a single one of the participants, the group nevertheless seems familiar to me. There is an insignificant young man, a rather portly older man, a hysterical young woman, no, I don't seem to have seen any of them before, but a strange feeling comes over me when I notice that one of the participants in the merrymaking secretly bends down and makes some notes on a tatty piece of paper that he drags out from some hiding place between his thighs.

Sitting swinging his legs on a high bar stool, I now discover the man whom I met on the beach earlier in the night. He is giving a lengthy lecture to those sitting around him, the spherical face with the many wrinkles is in constant motion and looks like a burst rubber ball that has been out in the rain for far too long. I don't want to disturb him, and he doesn't see me as his eyes are almost closed by his many wrinkles.

There are only three alcoves left now, and I have still not found the person I am looking for. In one of the alcoves I see my two tormenters from the beach, who have obviously chosen to continue their drinking in this dive. I hurry on, make myself as unnoticeable as possible in the hope that they won't catch sight of me and continue their tiring pursuit.

As I pass them, one of them raises his bottle to his lips and drinks from it.

'I'm putting my bottle to my lips and taking a mighty swig,' he tells himself.

'And at that moment he goes past and throws a quick glance at us,' bellows the other.

The last alcove is empty, as though it is waiting to receive the next lot of guests, but out of the next to the last appears Askaron. Without having seen me he goes over towards a door in the near end of the room.

'I go after him,' I murmur, before I can bite my tongue.

I follow him into the next room, which is even better lit, and where the company seems to be even more motley.

People are standing in groups, within each of which there may well be some movement, but nevertheless the constellations seem to be strangely fixed or lifeless. These characters have apparently had the idea of fooling the person entering, that is to say me, into believing that I am in a waxwork museum, while at the same time their flesh is creeping something awful.

Before I have managed to make contact with Askaron he has gone over to a girl standing alone as though expecting him. I take up a position as close as possible without being noticed, so as to observe his approach.

He holds out an inviting hand to her, but she draws back. He pretends to be uninterested, and makes a couple of nondescript remarks. She becomes ensnared by his words. He adds another casual comment which makes the girl fish for more.

I now take the liberty of getting so close to them that I can hear him telling some complicated story about a lonely girl who couldn't find an opportunity to show how kind she was. The girl is making swallowing movements, as though she is devouring his every word.

In addition to noting his technique, I observe that Askaron is devoting part of his attention to another member of the party. This is a cultured, rather reserved man whose only particular characteristic seems to be that he is keeping a ceaseless watch on a man with such interest that I can only assume he is shadowing the man in question. The person being shadowed, who is called Karon, is someone I have met before.

Probably to hide the fact that he is spying, the cultured man walks across to a girl. He behaves initially as though he knew her beforehand, but to no avail. Suddenly he changes his manner, assumes a superior air, seems not to consider her as more than a street girl. Obviously, he has realized that this behaviour cannot be made to harmonize with his otherwise cultured and respectable manner, for he again alters his behaviour just as suddenly as before. With the deepest respect, he now takes the girl's hand and kisses it, assuming a deferential bearing as though paying court to a countess. The girl appears not to be surprised at his changeable manner, but feels rather attracted by it.

For a time I have been so preoccupied by the detective's confusing behaviour that I have forgotten to observe Askaron. He is no longer telling his girl a story, as he was before; on the contrary, he is now quite forthcoming and seems to have benefitted from her friendship for a long time. But just as I am turning my attention to him, he changes his conduct. He assumes an arrogant mien and looks appraisingly at the girl, as though he were about to buy her, or at least to hire her for a while.

I find his manner quite effective, but begin now also to suspect a wider context.

The man I assume to be a detective has only taken his eyes off Karon when the girl to whom he himself is paying court occasionally demands all his attention. Askaron is showing great interest in the man being shadowed.

In the group to which he belongs, Karon is starting up an acquaintance with a girl. He is expressing himself with the help of some romantic gesticulations, he turns his languishing eyes on the girl, and cautiously he leads her across to a fountain situated in the middle of the room. They sit down on the edge, where a few drops of spray splash over them.

A girl has come across to me. I am so preoccupied with my observations that I am not interested in establishing closer contact with her. So I hurry to make use of Askaron's teaching, and begin to tell her a story, but in contrast to Askaron I arrange it in such a way that it keeps her at a distance from me. She takes up provocative positions in front of me, I pretend to devote myself to the complex story I am telling her, I introduce certain comments about a shameless girl, and that dampens her enthusiasm quite a lot.

By so doing I have the opportunity to follow the chain further. It is obvious to me that Karon has a good deal of his attention fixed on a man who is demonstrating his range of achievements for a girl. One moment he stands there with drooping shoulders and seems to be expounding some complicated theory. The next he is lifting a heavy floor-standing vase, raising it up several times in outstretched arms. When he has finished his demonstration, he beats himself gently on the chest.

This crumbling athlete seems to be concerned with another man whom I have previously met in the shops in Dahle. From this, I know he is called Ron. He is standing together with a pretty girl who apparently is about to leave him, but suddenly Ron goes unconcernedly and self-confidently across to a bookcase. Without hesitating he takes out a valuable book, goes back with it as though it were his own, and stuffs it down into the girl's bag. She laughs in surprise, and stays with him. They appear not to have noticed that the man with the floor-standing vase has not stopped spying on them for a single instant.

Suddenly, I am overwhelmed by a violent feeling of nausea, it feels as though my entire body is filled with some alien fluid, I have to exert myself enormously to move my limbs, which are stiff and inert like wax. With difficulty I stumble forward, look at random for some way out of this living museum. Stumble against a young couple making the girl drop the bag she is carrying, banging my head against a man with bristling hair who is standing pawing a girl, bumping into a man sitting unmotivated at a writing desk scrawling all over some papers from which a pungent odour of human beings is arising.

Suddenly, I am standing by a door. I rush out through it and immediately feel better. While trying to find myself, I shake my limbs a little, straighten myself up, tidy my hair, all the time watching to make sure that the door through which I have forced my way out remains shut.

Now, at last, I feel sufficiently strengthened to look around. With some regret I note that I have still not made my way out into the open. This room is rather more poorly lit than the previous one, but the people in whose company I now find myself, nevertheless seem to me to be more pleasant than those I have left, despite the fact that they certainly don't appear to be quite normal. In front of me stands a man holding his hand to his face. In a corner there is someone who seems to be trying to talk to himself, as he is constantly addressing comments to the wall. One man who is walking backwards, stopping now and again to look at the floor, is on the point of walking into me. I move, to sit down beside a man who has placed a screen between himself and the lamp on the table.

As I sit down my attention is caught by a woman entering the room. Calmly and naturally, she approaches me. She gives me a friendly look.

'Would you like me to help you to find the way out?' she says.